The Richest
Man in Babylon
Continued Stories

Also by Pauly Hart

Novels:
>By the Gates of the Garden of Eden

Short Horror:
>Becky!
>Mountain to Mountain
>Blood of the Pecos
>Superior Respondent
>Ouesso to Epena
>The Book of Lesser Voices
>Empire of the Dragon
>The Book of Lesser Voices

Fantastic History:
>The Word of Yahweh unto Enoch
>Tate's Hell: The Full Story

Theology:
>My Flat Earth
>Biblical Cosmology, (8+ languages)
>Please Kick Me Out of Your Church
>An Uncomfortable and Disastrous Creature

Finance:
>The Richest Man in Babylon Continued Stories
>Economic Alarm Clock: On the Brink of Your Financial Ruin

Poetry:
>Stupid Mind Tricks
>Book of Love and Laughter
>The Cross and the Poet
>What is Poep?
>I Love You More Than a Fox Loves Blueberries
>The Night Clerk Held a Broken Pencil
>Spontaneous Psalms
>Kicking the Prick

Collections:
>Sometimes I Write Tiny Stories
>Adelphoi
>Dreams Both Big and Small

Periodicals:
- Rush of Many Waters (1-20)
- Modern Epistle (1-8)
- Microzine (1-5)

Periodical Serials:
- The S.R.O.
- Kenny and the Azod Mythic
- Chip Flippers

Translations:
- The Testament of Job in Modern English
- Targum Jonathan Paraphrased: Genesis 1-25

With Co-Author Jennifer Hart:
- Adulting: A Daily Guide on Being an Adultier Adult

With children authors:
- Farrell Family Fables

Audio books:
- Biblical Cosmology
- Superior Respondent

Young Adult Fiction as Polly Little Deer (Pseudonym):
- Jenn Lynn: The Light Within, Book 1
- Jenn Lynn: Surrounding Darkness, Book 2

Children's Fiction as Mister Lee (Pseudonym):
- Koko the Dragon
- Orbs of the Over
- Saph the Adventurer
- Mathmagician and other Tales of Awesomeness
- Professor Bimples and the case of the Missing Wallet

All books are available on
Amazon.com and PaulyHart.com

The Richest
Man in Babylon
Continued Stories

by
Pauly Hart

ISBN: 978-1-955399-00-5

Library of Congress Catalog Data is available at: Loc.gov
This book is available at cost on Amazon.com and wherever fine books are sold.

Front cover design by Pauly Hart.
Editing Assistance by William G. Hart

Paperback version printed in Savannah, Georgia, USA, where available.

Second Edition, 2026

Author Contact: EmpiresAndGenerals@gmail.com
Author Website: PaulyHart.com

For
Katharine
Elias
And
Gideon

Ahead of you stretches your future like a road leading into the distance. Along that road are ambitions you wish to accomplish . . . desires you wish to gratify. To bring your ambitions and desires to fulfillment, you must be successful with money. Use the financial principles made clear in the pages which follow. Let them guide you away from the stringencies of a lean purse to that fuller, happier life a full purse makes possible. Like the law of gravity, they are universal and unchanging. May they prove for you, as they have proven to so many others, a sure key to a fat purse, larger bank balances and gratifying financial progress.

LO, MONEY IS PLENTIFUL
FOR THOSE WHO UNDERSTAND
THE SIMPLE RULES OF ITS ACQUISITION

1. Start thy purse to fattening
2. Control thy expenditures
3. Make thy gold multiply
4. Guard thy treasures from loss
5. Make of thy dwelling a profitable investment
6. Insure a future income
7. Increase thy ability to earn

From The Richest Man in Babylon
George S. Clason

Foreword

From <u>The Richest Man in Babylon</u>
George S. Clason

Our prosperity as a nation depends upon the personal financial prosperity of each of us as individuals. This book deals with the personal successes of each of us. Success means accomplishments as the result of our own efforts and abilities. Proper preparation is the key to our success. Our acts can be no wiser than our thoughts. Our thinking can be no wiser than our understanding. This book of cures for lean purses has been termed a guide to financial understanding. That, indeed, is its purpose: to offer those who are ambitious for financial success an insight which will aid them to acquire money, to keep money and to make their surpluses earn more money. In the pages which follow, we are taken back to Babylon, the cradle in which was nurtured the basic principles of finance now recognized and used the world over. To new readers the author is happy to extend the wish that its pages may contain for them the same inspiration for growing bank accounts, greater financial successes and the solution of difficult personal financial problems so enthusiastically reported by readers from coast to coast.

To the business executives who have distributed these tales in such generous quantities to friends, relatives, employees and associates, the author takes this opportunity to express his gratitude. No endorsement could be higher than that of practical men who appreciate its teachings because they, themselves, have worked up to important successes by applying the very principles it advocates. Babylon became the wealthiest city of the ancient world because its citizens were the richest people of their time. They appreciated the value of money. They practiced sound financial principles in acquiring money, keeping money and making their money earn more money. They provided for themselves what we all desire . . . incomes for the future.

Preface

There I was, age ten, hunkered down under the pew at church, trying to tune out the boring sermon and read the Bible. I was all over the place, skipping here and there, trying to absorb the whole things in one sitting. The Protestant Canon is 70 books (Psalms being 5) and is a tome of great magnitude. A collection of history, poetry, law, war, census records, gore, and sex. I'm surprised my parents let me have one at all.

But they valued the teachings that came out of it. My mother was the daughter of Baptist missionaries and my father was also of the Baptist persuasion. They were making both sets of their parents unhappy by attending a Charismatic church. There was lots of stuff... Holy Rolling, Speaking in Tongues, Faith Healing., but at the heart of it all was this rated X book. And they let me read it without getting spanked.

I was happy. Although it wasn't <u>Lord of the Rings</u>, <u>The Stainless Steel Rat</u>, or <u>Choose Your Own Adventure</u> - it kept me up at night thinking about cool stuff. Mostly, I loved to read... Anything really... Even if it was just <u>The King James Version of The Holy Bible</u>. To be honest, I read <u>The Story of Ferdinand</u> when I was three and haven't stopped reading since. One of my earliest Mentors, Keith Wheeler told me "You absorb books."

I've written a lot of books. This, if I'm correct, will be my 34th. Most are collections of essays or poems or short stories. I've written "the" novel and several novelettes and novellas. This is probably one of them... Except that it's a self-help book maybe? Oh. My wife and I wrote one of those too. It's actually pretty cool. But I digress...

When I first thought about writing this book, it was on the heels of reading and listening to <u>The Richest Man in</u>

Babylon on audiobook four times in a row. I was enamored with the story devices that George Clason employed. I loved the way the characters seemed to jump out of the page at me. George's characters invited me into their world in a way that few others had. I had a deep desire to hear more of what the characters had to say to me. As there was no more material available, I found that I might write the material myself, soas to appease my own inner desires.

The original version of George's book was published in 1926 and then renewed in 1963. According to the dates, April the 8th, 2021 ended the copyright on the book, according to U.S. Law. I procrastinated much in writing the book you have before you today, but I have been working on the "Laws" found within for quite some time. Most of them are things that were taught to me, as well as things that I have learned in Real Estate, in the Stock and Crypto markets, and things I've picked up owning and managing businesses. There have been a lot of those.

I plan on writing "More Continued Stories" featuring the other characters in the original book not listed in this one. I have a lot in store for the continuing world of George Clason's Babylon. I hope I can do him justice with my "Laws" - I also hope I can do you justice with them.

I have many people to thank for the ideas in this book. My first and third wives, William George Hart, JB Farrell, Dan Kerkoff, Jeff Johns, Keith Wheeler, Rich Mullins, Pete Walker, Mike Grbic, and others. There are too many to name so let me end the list there. As stated in the book: "A smart man learns from his own mistakes but a wise man learns from the mistakes of others. Long have I sought after the "Teachable Spirit" and hopefully one day, I will get there.

With all that being said, I will refrain from writing too much longer in this Preface.

I trust you enjoy the lessons and the stories that are offered here.

There is much wisdom in understanding the keys to wealth that George Clason had to offer.

And, by the way, If you haven't George S. Clason's book The Richest Man in Babylon and are reading this first, you are going to not have much fun. You will get lost in the context and wonder why I'm using some archaic English.

Go pick it up or read it free online. I've got a copy at PaulyHart.com

-Pauly Hart
April, 2021

An Historical Sketch of Babylon

From <u>The Richest Man in Babylon</u>
George S. Clason

In the pages of history there lives no city more glamorous than Babylon. Its very name conjures visions of wealth and splendor. Its treasures of gold and jewels were fabulous. One naturally pictures such a wealthy city as located in a suitable setting of tropical luxury, surrounded by rich natural resources of forests, and mines. Such was not the case. It was located beside the Euphrates River, in a flat, arid valley. It had no forests, no mines—not even stone for building. It was not even located upon a natural trade-route. The rainfall was insufficient to raise crops.

Babylon is an outstanding example of man's ability to achieve great objectives, using whatever means are at his disposal. All of the resources supporting this large city were man-developed. All of its riches were man-made. Babylon possessed just two natural resources—a fertile soil and water in the river. With one of the greatest engineering accomplishments of this or any other day, Babylonian engineers diverted the waters from the river by means of dams and immense irrigation canals. Far out across that arid valley went these canals to pour the life giving waters over the fertile soil. This ranks among the first engineering feats known to history. Such abundant crops as were the reward of this irrigation system the world had never seen before.

Fortunately, during its long existence, Babylon was ruled by successive lines of kings to whom conquest and plunder were but incidental. While it engaged in many wars, most of these were local or defensive against ambitious conquerors from other countries who coveted the fabulous treasures of Babylon. The outstanding rulers of Babylon live in history because of their wisdom, enterprise and justice. Babylon produced no strutting monarchs who sought to conquer the known world that all nations might pay homage to their egotism.

As a city, Babylon exists no more. When those energizing human forces that built and maintained the city for thousands of years were withdrawn, it soon became a deserted ruin. The site of the city is in Asia about six hundred miles east of the Suez Canal, just north of the Persian Gulf. The latitude is about thirty degrees above the Equator, practically the same as that of Yuma, Arizona. It possessed a climate similar to that of this American city, hot and dry.

Today, this valley of the Euphrates, once a populous irrigated farming district, is again a windswept arid waste. Scant grass and desert shrubs strive for existence against the windblown sands. Gone are the fertile fields, the mammoth cities and the long caravans of rich merchandise. Nomadic bands of Arabs, securing a scant living by tending small herds, are the only inhabitants. Such it has been since about the beginning of the Christian era.

Dotting this valley are earthen hills. For centuries, they were considered by travelers to be nothing else. The attention of archaeologists were finally attracted to them because of broken pieces of pottery and brick washed down by the occasional rain storms. Expeditions, financed by European and American museums, were sent here to excavate and see what could be found. Picks and shovels soon proved these hills to be ancient cities. City graves, they might well be called.

Babylon was one of these. Over it for something like twenty centuries, the winds had scattered the desert dust. Built originally of brick, all exposed walls had disintegrated and gone back to earth once more. Such is Babylon, the wealthy city, today. A heap of dirt, so long abandoned that no living person even knew its name until it was discovered by carefully removing the refuse of centuries from the streets and the fallen wreckage of its noble temples and palaces.

Many scientists consider the civilization of Babylon and other cities in this valley to be the oldest of which there is a definite record. Positive dates have been proved reaching back 8000 years. An interesting fact in this connection is the means used to determine these dates. Uncovered in the ruins of Babylon were descriptions of an eclipse of the sun. Modern astronomers readily computed the time when such an eclipse, visible in Babylon, occurred and thus established a known relationship between their calendar and our own.

In this way, we have proved that 8000 years ago, the Sumerites, who inhabited Babylonia, were living in walled cities. One can only conjecture for how many centuries previous such cities had existed. Their inhabitants were not mere barbarians living within protecting walls. They were an educated and enlightened people. So far as written history goes, they were the first engineers, the first astronomers, the first mathematicians, the first financiers and the first people to have a written language.

Mention has already been made of the irrigation systems which transformed the arid valley into an agricultural paradise. The remains of these canals can still be traced, although they are mostly filled with accumulated sand. Some of them were of such size that, when empty of water, a dozen horses could be ridden abreast along their bottoms. In size they compare favorably with the largest canals in Colorado and Utah.

In addition to irrigating the valley lands, Babylonian engineers completed another project of similar magnitude. By means of an elaborate drainage system they reclaimed an immense area of swamp land at the mouths of the Euphrates and Tigris Rivers and put this also under cultivation. Herodotus, the Greek traveler and historian, visited Babylon while it was in its prime and has given us the only known description by an outsider. His writings give a graphic description of the city and some of the unusual customs of its people. He mentions the remarkable fertility of the soil and the bountiful harvest of wheat and barley which they produced.

The glory of Babylon has faded but its wisdom has been preserved for us. For this we are indebted to their form of records. In that distant day, the use of paper had not been invented. Instead, they laboriously engraved their writing upon tablets of moist clay. When completed, these were baked and became hard tile. In size, they were about six by eight inches, and an inch in thickness.

These clay tablets, as they are commonly called, were used much as we use modern forms of writing. Upon them were engraved legends, poetry, history, transcriptions of royal decrees, the laws of the land, titles to property, promissory notes and even letters which were dispatched by messengers to distant cities. From these clay tablets we are permitted an insight into the intimate, personal affairs of the people. For example, one tablet, evidently from the records of a country storekeeper, relates that upon the given date a certain named customer brought in a cow and exchanged it for seven sacks of wheat, three being delivered at the time and the other four to await the customer's pleasure. Safely buried in the wrecked cities, archaeologists have recovered entire libraries of these tablets, hundreds of thousands of them.

One of the outstanding wonders of Babylon was the immense walls surrounding the city. The ancients ranked them with the great pyramid of Egypt as belonging to the "seven wonders of the world." Queen Semiramis is credited with having erected the first walls during the early history of the city. Modern excavators have been unable to find any trace of the original walls. Nor is their exact height known. From mention made by early writers, it is estimated they were about fifty to sixty feet high, faced on the outer side with burnt brick and further protected by a deep moat of water.

The later and more famous walls were started about six hundred years before the time of Christ by King Nabopolassar. Upon such a gigantic scale did he plan the rebuilding, he did not live to see the work finished. This was left to his son, Nebuchadnezzar, whose name is familiar in Biblical history. The height and length of these later walls staggers belief. They are reported upon reliable authority to have been about one hundred and sixty feet high, the equivalent of the height of a modern fifteen story office building. The total length is estimated as between nine and eleven miles. So wide was the top that a six-horse chariot could be driven around them. Of this tremendous structure, little now remains except portions of the foundations and the moat. In addition to the ravages of the elements, the Arabs completed the destruction by quarrying the brick for building purposes elsewhere.

Against the walls of Babylon marched, in turn, the victorious armies of almost every conqueror of that age of wars of conquest. A host of kings laid siege to Babylon, but always in vain. Invading armies of that day were not to be considered lightly. Historians speak of such units as 10,000 horsemen, 25,000 chariots, 1200 regiments of foot soldiers with 1000 men to the regiment. Often two or three years of preparation would be required to assemble war materials and depots of food along the proposed line of march.

The city of Babylon was organized much like a modern city. There were streets and shops. Peddlers offered their wares through residential districts. Priests officiated in magnificent temples. Within the city was an inner enclosure for the royal palaces. The walls about this were said to have been higher than those about the city.

The Babylonians were skilled in the arts. These included sculpture, painting, weaving, gold working and the manufacture of metal weapons and agricultural implements. Their Jewelers created most artistic jewelry. Many samples have been recovered from the graves of its wealthy citizens and are now on exhibition in the leading museums of the world.

At a very early period when the rest of the world was still hacking at trees with stone-headed axes, or hunting and fighting with flint-pointed spears and arrows, the Babylonians were using axes, spears and arrows with metal heads.

The Babylonians were clever financiers and traders. So far as we know, they were the original inventors of money as a means of exchange, of promissory notes and written titles to property. Babylon was never entered by hostile armies until about 540 years before the birth of Christ. Even then the walls were not captured. The story of the fall of Babylon is most unusual. Cyrus, one of the great conquerors of that period, intended to attack the city and hoped to take its impregnable walls.

Advisors of Nabonidus, the King of Babylon, persuaded him to go forth to meet Cyrus and give him battle without waiting for the city to be besieged. In the succeeding defeat to the Babylonian army, it fled away from the city. Cyrus, thereupon, entered the open gates and took possession without resistance.

Thereafter the power and prestige of the city gradually waned until, in the course of a few hundred years, it was eventually abandoned, deserted, left for the winds and storms to level once again to that desert earth from which its grandeur had originally been built. Babylon had fallen, never to rise again, but to it civilization owes much.

The eons of time have crumbled to dust the proud walls of its temples, but the wisdom of Babylon endures.

Money is the medium by which earthly success is measured.

Money makes possible the enjoyment of the best the earth affords.

Money is plentiful for those who understand the simple laws which govern its acquisition.

Money is governed today by the same laws which controlled it when prosperous men thronged the streets of Babylon, six thousand years ago.

1

Bansir the Chariot Builder

Bansir, the chariot builder of Babylon, looked around the workshop for the last time. In front of him was where he had built chariot after chariot, year after year. Next to the workshop was his simple house, where he had lived a number of comfortable years with his wife and children. Around it lay the low wall where he had once sat and contemplated his destiny. His sons were packing up his last belongings. Nahmbir, his oldest, came to stand beside him.

"All is almost ready." He stated, looking around with his father. "Soon you will away to thy new home." A hearty clap on the back and he walked away. But Bansir still stood, looking out at the little shop with reflection. It seemed almost yesterday that he and his wife had little to eat and little work in front of them. Wealth had come back then, one job at a time, and once he was done with a chariot, he would have to wait until the next job shown itself to work yet again.

He remembers that day with clarity. Remembers the slaves with their water buckets walking by, remembers Kobbi asking for two shekels, remembers going to see Arkad and what had transpired thereafter. For it was their small meeting with Arkad and his stories that had sparked a seed of faith inside of Bansir. It was that day that had changed Bansir forever. For what else could it have been, but that very meeting with the richest man of Babylon? What else could it have been? Kobbi had come by to ask for a loan for the noblemen's feast, so that he might procure for himself some oils for his lyre and a new hat.

Indeed it was, not some time after that, after hearing the words of Arkad, that he had laid hold of his wisdom with such ferocity, many had thought Bansir under a spell. Rather cheerfully had he picked up his hammer once he and Kobbi had returned from the meeting with Arkad that he worked well into the night and finished the chariot the very next morrow. His own words rang back into his mind, from that day: "Consider, also, our sons. Need they be content to banquet upon sour goat's milk and porridge?"

And on that next day, delivering the chariot to the rich customer had he saved not one tenth, but one fifth of his earnings? For he had a dire need to quicken his life's wealth to match that life's wasted wealth misspent in his younger years. His purse had always been lean and the best way to fatten it was to become leaner than the purse until it fattened beyond his own rotund waste. Starve the body, feed the wallet. For until the fateful day that Kobbi and he had gone to Arkad, when there was excess, it was spent on such small luxuries as anything that caught the eye. Roast pork, aurochs ear, salmon, trout and once, a gomer of Egyptian barley for his wife. But after there was feast, ever was there the inevitable famine. For as a trifle that was laid before them, they would gobble it up as soon as it was placed on their larder.

But these last purposefully lean years since had made their mark upon his purse, as well as his tunic. He had never tied his belt so tightly as he had in those days.

"Lo! Who is this man awasting away?" One of his customers called to him. "And have you seen Bansir?" Oh how they had laughed at him. But laugh they would and did, but did not know the secrets laid beneath his bed, secrets that were small and round and gold and wonderful to keep. And so it was that after three years of savings that he found he could not sleep. He asked others about saving and they told him how to invest instead.

"Why do you love slow gold?" one of them asked. "For gold that sits still is slow. When it moves in investment, it grows so much the quicker. Or if you prefer not to lose sight of your gold, then have you thought about increasing your own business?"

Bansir had heeded the man's advice and took all of his gold from under his bed and opened another shop. He managed the shop well and they began to make not only chariots, but horse tack, donkey tack, camel bags, oxen yokes, and other items that one needs when you own animals.

And so it was, seven years of investing later, after the first three of saving, that Bansir came to a place in his destiny where he had two choices which seemed equally viable. But he was growing older and did not want to stretch leather or hew wood until he died. He found that he was an able manager of workers... So much so that he could train, supervise, and keep track of up to twenty men. His oldest son, also was quite as good as he, and sought to make his own fortune. He was puzzled by what to do.

And so it came to his mind to visit Arkad, who still kept up school for the king, and did ask Arkad how he may invest the remainder of his years, and if he had any ideas on the decision that loomed before him. He had in his mind to bring Kobbi, his oldest friend. So he fetched for him and they both went to see Arkad, in the Temple of Learning.

"Oh ho ho, my old friend Bansir," cried Arkad, upon seeing him. "And how do you now? Is your purse fatter than you used to be?"

"Yea, it is as you say good sir," replied Bansir. "The purse is fat, and I am indeed a mere wisp of the fat man that you met ten years ago."

"Aha!" Ejaculated Arkad. "But it has not seemed like that long ago. For it was around this time that I had just started this great school here. And yet I did not see you in school with the other merchants and traders. How is it that... Wait! And yet, now I do recall! Yes it was in that same time that you, Kobbi, and many others came to me and asked that I either share my riches with you or give you my blessing."

"There were those that did that, yes it is true, for many a scoundrel still calls me friend. But what I do recall were your words and that they have laid ahold of my heart and changed me."

"Oh? Eh, what words did I speak to you then? For I confess, I have spoken more words that I can remember. Come now, do not be afraid. Tell me the truth."

Bansir paused and reflected for a moment. Was it indeed so very long ago that Arkad had spoken to them that he had now forgotten his very words that had so shaped his life? He proceeded, thinking this was but a test from his old friend.

"The three things you said to me that day will forever be in my mind my old friend," Bansir began, "for they are truer to me even on this day, than they ever were before." Bansir looked around and spied a small stool, walked over to it, grabbed it up, sat down and continued. "Now mind you, we had come to you, myself and Kobbi, Torfir, Lamkiel, Uzmet, Sinjar, and several others… All friends from your youth to ask you the simple question of how you gained your wealth and why it was that the gods had favored thee so. But you do not know why we came to you so I will tell it first."

Arkad, a glimmer in his eye, smiled and wrung his hands with anticipation. "Pray, do tell, for my attention now is as high as it has ever been."

Bansir continued.

"It was the mid-morning on that fateful day, the same day from which I had awoken from a dream of sorts… Nay, it was a fantasy sent to me by the very gods themselves, for what transpired thereafter was nothing short of the workings of the gods… It was in this fantasy that I saw the Bansir that could have been. From my belt hung a handsome purse, heavy with much coin. My wife was happy. She and I strode carelessly throughout the markets buying this and that – whatever our eyes spied, we purchased. We had the marketmen lay them all up on their donkeys and camels and take them back to our dwelling -Which was almost like a palace. Thus was my dream. Now this may seem like a trifle of a dream, a sorry one at best, but it was the feelings the coins in my purse produced which drove me almost mad that day."

Kobbi, having long held his tongue, encouraged him.

"Oh pray go on, old friend! Tell our dear Arkad which thou didst feel! You dally so long I can barely endure it!"

Laughter sprang out from many of the men around, for indeed, a crowd had been slowly gathering, seeing Bansir and his friends talking to Arkad.

Bansir grinned at his oldest and truest of friends. "Kobbi can testify to the story that I was distraught beyond all measure that day from the dream. For in that dream I had been the happiest that I had ever been in the whole of my life. I had no cares, no worries, no sense of impending calamity. For in life to that point all I had known was toil. Hands, back, feet, knees... All sore and splintering, all day and every day. But in my dream, I was hale and free. So much in the throes of joy was I that when I awoke, I was angry at the dream and scarce did much work all morning. For it was not soon thereafter that Kobbi came to me to borrow two shekels that I gave him this very same story."

"And march to you we did that very same instance." Kobbi declared, relieved that Bansir had finished this part of his tale. "But press on, good friend. You still have yet to tell our friend of younger years what he told us that day! Or shall I be the one on your behalf to do it?"

Bansir held up his hand. "Nay, though thy tales be beyond measure and your voice sweeter, I fear that there would be much nonsense interwoven inside of the tale. I will tell it."

More laughter from those around. Many had heard Kobbi's songs and knew well his art of embellishment. For in his tales if there had been, say, one farmer with one sheep… Kobbi would tell it as twenty farmers with thousands of sheep.

Bansir continued to his very patient listener. "When we came to you that day, it was driven by my desire, my heat, my longing to find out if that dream would or could ever be a reality. But it was when Kobbi did visit me that he stated that he had seen you earlier that morn and you didst acknowledge him with a grand salute, to his immense pleasure. Then Kobbi suggested that we might find you on that day and get from you the secrets of our lowly estates. That we brought our friends from yesteryear was also his idea. I sought to find out how my income so quickly flowed through my fingers and yours did not."

Kobbi was indignant. "For the love of all the gods and the priests who sing their praises, tell the man what he told you!"

Even more laughter than before erupted from the crowd of onlookers. One man, while eating a piece of bread with some milk, almost fainted, for he began choking.

When all was quiet once again Arkad prompted. "Pray finish thy tale, old friend… For it seems that the patience of your listeners is not your ally this day." He smiled.

Bansir nodded. He had wanted to relay this to Arkad, as he needed to drive the point home to him just how important Arkad's words had been, for it had changed Bansir in his most deepest parts.

"You told us all the story of Old Algamish and how you broke your back writing for him a copy of The Ninth Law. You told us of Azmur the brick maker and of Agger the shield maker, and of the wantonness of the minds of Old Algamish's sons. These stories you told us true, but it is the lessons that most stuck with me. For my mind is like a pit one digs for a lion. Once something gets inside of it, it cannot get out, lest I loose it myself. For in the first story of the bargain with Algamish, you labored long into the night, and on the morrow he told you the secret that began your journey."

Arkad's eyebrows were raised high, excited with anticipation.

"That the first secret that started you on your journey is this – To pay yourself first. And that it had not occurred to you before that day that you did not pay yourself first. For as you said in your youth, you panted hard after the lustful things that all youths do, and lived every turn of the moon, the allowance you received from your employer was soon spent by the next time he paid you again, if not before."

Kobbi clapped his hands, so excited was he with the final ending so soon in sight. Arkad waved him down, allowing Bansir to conclude.

"The second secret that you gave to us, I believe was in the telling of the tale itself. That you took Algamish at his word at all was the mark of a true learner, and that was what I wished to be from the very day I heard you. That you listened to those who knew more about money than you did. That you sought the advice of the rich and then did as they instructed was the second lesson I took from your story, for you said: 'Therefore did I decide to find out how one might accumulate wealth, and when I had found out, to make this my task and do it well.' And so you took the knowledge of Old Algamish and made it your own."

"The third is like it," Bansir started before Kobbi could interrupt him, "That the gold coins I make are my children, and my children may have also their own children, and when the gold's children's children are making more than I am, then I may spend my time working with my gold and not my hands. This is the true measure of wealth, as I have learned from you. That my time, that my energy, that the works of my hands saw and hew the works of the chariot, but that in the measure of time, that my time and energy are concerned with the workings of my money."

Arkad's laughter and clapping erupted like a child's. So much so was his joy that he jumped up and danced around for a goodly while before settling back down. Many were amazed at the sprightliness of his gait and the manner in which he carried himself. He dropped back to his cushion and breathed a sigh.

"You have made more use of the little that I have given than many of the rich merchants and appointees that have entered into my lectures, and to them have I given everything!" Arkad declared with another burst of laughter. "To think all this time, it was people like you who should have been in attendance!"

The crowd stirred a little at this. Many of the men there were in attendance at Arkad's school. They had heard his "Seven Cures" and "Five Laws" lectures and had seen increase in their own businesses. Many of them knew of Bansir, but he had never attended the school. At seeing the men, Kobbi spoke up.

"Good men of Babylon, think not that our dear friend Bansir has taken something which was not freely given to each of you. For indeed, he is the friend of my boyhood days. We have spent a lifetime together. That he is the most stolid and tenacious of men is beyond doubt, for he has been my steadfast rock in my whole life. Whereas I, flitting here and there to each new party... I have been his source of entertainment, and perchance, his vicarious source of mirth, so little doeth the man smile. Where he would not go to a street corner and ply his music, I would. Where I would not work long hours in sweaty work, he would. It is the manner in which I know this man to tell you in an utmost certainty that he is no scoundrel and means every word that comes out of his mouth. For it was of a highest certainty that when he learned these three things, he applied them with all diligence."

"It is true." Bansir agreed. "When I did hear your words, Arkad, I went home and finished the chariot I had been procrastinating on and when I delivered it to the rich man, I paid myself first. And not ten percent did I pay, but twenty. For I was late to the wealth parade and should do my best to catch up. My wife and children did not understand the mood I had been in when we went through the market. For the gold I had brought with me was a mere 80% of the total gold he had paid me with. And from that total percentage I needed to pay back a small loan that I had taken out from Mathon, the gold lender. And also, at that very moment, I had decided not to take out any more loans, so that one half of my total was dedicated to buy supplies for the next chariots build. So when I told my wife that we were only allotted four fifths of my total earnings to spend that day on things at the market to live on, until the next time I was paid again, I thought with a great certainty that she would take the children and leave me then and there."

"But you must tend after your family!" Someone in the crowd stated. Others murmured their agreement.

"Tend after them I do!" Bansir said angrily. "Just not to their expectation of great comfort... And that was on that day, not every day since then. Do you not recall the Wedding Festival that I threw for my son, not eight moons ago? Yes. When we celebrate, we do not have any lack. For we save up for the celebration in the times of labor, and invest heavily with every payment. But that is not the point of this... Nor is it the point that loans are a bad bargain. Many a person has been saved by a loan. But it is better to loan to yourself in the future, than take a loan from a stranger." Bansir concluded.

"And look at him now," Kobbi declared. "Today he is leaving his old home and moving to Nineveh. His shop will remain, with his son in charge and hired laborers to make new chariots here in Babylon, his new shop in Susa, and his daily dealings with the woodsmen, tanners and bronze workers… He is indeed a wealthy man!"

Murmurs and whispers were around them from the men.

"We did not know you were so wealthy!" One of them said.

"Nor did I!" Bansir exclaimed, eyes wide, directed at Kobbi. "I simply kept applying the wisdom that I learned. I saw the need for a shop in Susa, so I found the most talented builder there, supplied him, and he pays me the earnings, after his salary and expenses. To tell truth, I have done the same in Erech and Opis… Yet I do not think Kobbi knew of this. But you men, you also have done things of this nature? Saw the need and filled it with your expertise? For I tell you the truth: My shops in other towns are the children of my gold, and their earnings are the children of their children. This is why I must go to Nineveh and seek to expand my gold into more ground. For in Nineveh I can make chariots for our King's new palace at Dur Sharrukin. It is the easiest of decisions, though my heart is divided, I do not want to leave Babylon. I will not only leave all of my friends behind, but my eldest son and his children, who will watch over the original shop here. When the time is right, I will journey to the great abyss below and he will carry on my work for me."

All were quiet as Bansir's story came to an end..

"Every fool must learn." Bansir stated. "That was what Old Algamish told you, my old friend. And so, I, the biggest fool of them all for so long, have learned. And that is the reason that I come here today before I leave for Nineveh. You, Arkad, who once showed me how a slow-witted chariot maker might do well in life, do now have the power over the remainder of my destiny. Nahmbir, my oldest son, thinks it wise for me to go to Nineveh to increase our fortune... But what say you, I wonder? For this is the real reason that I have laid bare my increases to you. All know that your words have such power over men and their wealth. Now all know about my wealth, but I would know more."

Bansir's humility and plea did not fall on Arkad without effect. Arkad arose and beckoned Bansir to rise also. Placing his hands about him, he embraced him as a kinsman. That doing, he began to speak.

"Hear now, oh men of Babylon, for such is the tale of a common man now made master over his own destiny. I do recall more and more of this encounter so long ago with Bansir, Kobbi and their friends... Indeed we did attend school together and listen to the wise priests at Temple. We did share in our youths together but from there we did each go our separate way into adulthood. Has it been easy, this course in life? Has it been easy on our new much thinned friend Bansir to save instead of please his wife in her immediate desires? Was it easy for me to labor long in the night, hunched over the tablets? No? Certainly some of you must think so for the scorning you are now showing Bansir?"

He looked around the room, catching each of their eyes.

"Far from it! For because you did not know Bansir had made for himself this small fortune, you only assumed that he may be doing poorly, because of his thinning frame. You assumed because you saw more and more workers doing his work for him that you thought him fragile or sickly. How when he was away for more than a day, out of the city gates, that you thought him spending his money on selfish delights or women? And because of these assumptions on your part none of you put together the truth. That among your lesser, arose from you one more powerful than you. That because of his dedication to learning the laws of wealth, he arose taller than all of us. For in ten years he has done this. Many of you started from where he was from the inheritance your fathers built from you and you are mostly the same. Many of you so called mighty men, are but ants in the luminescence of this towering giant who stands before you with the humility of a beggar."

Bansir sought to sit down, mindful of the attention he was getting, but Arkad held him, arm under shoulder, as a brother.

"Behold oh men of Babylon. One of your own, who was never invited to the King's Teaching Room. Who was never invited to the Palace, who was never in attendance at your parties or at your gatherings on wealth-building. Behold how his purse outweighs your own."

So saying, Arkad let Bansir sit down. Bansir's face, redder than the sunset, eyes fixed on the ground. Yet Arkad was not done speaking.

"It appears that our good friend Bansir, and also Kobbi, from what I see, did well to heed my words. They saved and invested and their wealth-trees are overladen with much fruit. But they have not eaten their fruit, but instead, planted more fruit in different fields. And is it not so that daily do I walk through the market and see one of Kobbi's students plying his songs on the corner? And not just one corner, but several? And do I not pass by Kobbi's school on the way to Temple? For both of them have done what could have been done by any of you. Plant and sow, plant and sow... For in this way they have built for themselves orchards and vineyards in their own name, to give to their children and to their children's children."

"And as for advice my dearest of old friends, Bansir, for this is what I call you now, knowing your mind is as resolute as mine own... Do what you think is best for your wealth orchard... For indeed as a ratio of the matter, it may be larger than most here. So how would I begin to tell you about chariot building? If you recall, I only ask the advice of brick making from brick makers! Go! Go! Go to Nineveh, for you have my blessing and also my encouragement! And tell me if you need investors for more of your projects! My own gold needs fertile soil, and in you I see the essence of the maturity of a wealth stream that may water plenty."

Bansir left for Nineveh that day, leaving behind his eldest son, his legacy, and a smile in Arkad's heart.

2

Kalabab the Camel Trader

Kalabab the camel trader laid his weary head down on the rug, inside the tent facing Babylon. For many years he had traveled these roads, and now, again, here he was at the gates of the jewel that he loved so very, very well. "Oh Babylon, Babylon," he thought to himself. "However have I loved thee." He closed his eyes and dozed a little. When he awoke, he was surrounded by sounds. His men had kept their promise.

"Old man!" cried Vuruk, "are you dead or merely sleeping?!" The rough desert man came into the tent and took off his turban. His long black hair flowed down onto his shoulders, wet with the sweat of his journey. "You appear as thine own youth does escape thee." Vuruk said. "Shall we carry thee into the city on your bed so that thou may pay homage to Marduk and the other gods before thou doest perish from age?" He plopped down roughly by Kalabab, smiling.

Kalabab managed a laugh. "Behold, I am not dead yet. Are the rest of the men with you?" Kalabab asked. "It wouldst do me well to hear of their journeys."

"As I am the first to arrive, I know not of the others... But what of mine own journey? Am I to you but a mere dog that thou would ignore my needs?" Vuruk scowled but then quickly laughed. "Ah! Be of good cheer you old goat. Your fortune lies with us tonight, and not in some grave… You have time yet to hear my tale, such as it is." Vuruk stood and began to walk out. "I have yet to pitch my tent. We will start a fire! I have a goat to skin!" And with that, he left.

It was well after sunset when Kalabab emerged from his tent. The goat was on the fire and the company was cutting it up amongst themselves. Upon seeing Kalabab arrive at the fire, a great cheering went up from each of them. They set him at a high perched rug upon pillows and offered him beer from Lower Egypt and goat from one of the herds of Elipypes, for he had brought many. The cool wind blew at them from the North-East, a rare thing this time of year, but in the desert it can go from heat to freezing as the sun makes her retreat across the vault of the heavens. Vuruk, the tall swarthy man who had been Kalabab's chief packer all those years had been the first to arrive. Richa Atad, the Nubian, also was there in fine red and gray robes. Faroud, from north of Scythia, gleaming with his pale skin and lightish hair. Polcepias, the Greek sat quietly. Tartak the Akkadian from Ur. And finally there was Elipypes, the small eyed man with straight dark hair. Kalabab ate and drank with them and was merry. All men exchanged small speech, waiting on Kalabab to speak.

When he was through eating, Kalabab put his skewer in the fire and began.

"There were twenty seven of you dogs the last time I saw you and we sat upon this same hill overlooking Babylon. That was ten years ago and my weary bones would have been laid to rest well before yesterday but for the hope and happiness that my heart should endure upon seeing you now. And see you I have, but question the number remaining. I do count but six of you men who served with me last, besides myself, and our servants."

"Recall what I made you promise me years ago. That when I told you of the laws of gold, taught to me by Nomasir, son of Arkad, The Richest Man in Babylon, you would return to me, on this very night, ten years later, and tell me what you have done with yourself. This promise you all made before I paid you on that very next morning. For only Vuruk stayed with me after, and as my chief packer, worked with me another five years when I was too tired from my own labors, and quit my business, selling him the majority of it."

"A cheat ! A cheat!" Faroud, the lean light skinned man cried. Vuruk threw a piece of bread at him and hit him squarely on the nose.

"Not so!" Vuruk cried out, laughing. "I am a just an honorable man!"

One of the others, Richa Atad, a dark skinned man, shoved Faroud backwards and they began to grapple.

"I daresay that the years have laid upon your minds much foolishness if you behave this way even now." Kalabab chided.

Faroud, having gained the upper hand, sat on Richa Atad's chest and replied. "No master Kalabab, for it is just that I have missed this son-of-a-dog so much in that long time." He laughed and got off him.

"You are all still dogs." Vuruk scolded them. "Even as you were when you worked under me for the master."

"And were you not just as they were, not so long ago?" Kalabab asked.

Vuruk said nothing, but bit into another piece of goat and stared into the fire.

The spitting of grease from the goat over the fire spattered and hissed. All around them were their separate camps. A massive collection of working men's laughter, crackling fires, neighing horses, braying donkeys, snorting camels, and bleating sheep assaulted their ears. The stars shone gloriously, for it was a new moon and there were no clouds.

"With my working of the numbers, and as there are six of you sitting here, it comes out that one out of five of you from the former twenty seven has made it back to tell of their successes." Kalabab said to them. "Slim numbers. You recalled my tale that night, and you have made good on your promise to return. The ones that have not returned have either forgotten, or are too ashamed, or have been taken down to the abyss."

"Or mayhap are too rich to care?" Taratak said. Kalabab remembered him only vaguely. He had been but a boy then.

"Nay, they would have returned, for only to gloat over us. If they were indeed that rich, they would have set up booths last week and charged us all rent to stay on this hill." Elipypes said with a sly smile.

Vuruk laughed aloud as did the others. "Now why did not I think of this?" Vuruk declared, jumping to his feet. "But it is not too late! Come! Each of you! Give me now five shekels each for your hindquarters on my sand!" He laughed even louder than before.

Kalabab laughed as well. After a few moments of playful fighting he addressed them again.

"The sons of men ignore the wisdom and waste gold. I do not know of the other men who were with you that night, as it was a special night for me. I had come to realize that I should have been telling this story to all my caravan workers. But as it was, I only told it once and then not after again. It may have been as The Spirit gave me the utterance, but I do not know why I only told it to you. But look at you now. You are men of gold. Men of wisdom, strength, and honor. It pleases me much to be among your company, so great a horde of traders and merchants that you have become."

"Hear the armies of your employed men. Hear the many sounds that your animals make. Such is the sound of wealth. Such is the sound of the freedom that wealth brings. For it is not security that we seek, but freedom. And freedom comes when there is no want of gold."

They murmured agreement to this.

Recall if you will the bargain that Nomasir made with his father. For ten years wise Arkad sent him to acquire his own wealth, and so also I have made the same bargain with each of you. It has been ten years since I sealed you with this command, and now comes your accounting. For Nomasir was a rich man when he returned to his father ten years later, and indeed richer still when I met him, and so you too also, I suspect are richer than the last time I saw you."

"Remember what I learned and what the son of the richest man in Babylon told me. Gold comes easily and in increasing quantity to the person who saves at least 1/10th of their earnings. Gold labors diligently and multiplies for the person who finds it profitable employment. Gold clings to the protection of the person who invests their gold with wise people. Gold slips away from the person who invests gold into purposes through which they are not familiar. Gold flees the person who tries to force it into impossible earnings."

"I ask you this: has gold come or labored or clung to you? And in what ways were you tempted to have gold flee or slip away? So then let us hear your stories," Kalabab said. "And do not regale us with lists of travels. Tell us only what matters. For storytelling is like the fine wine of the Phoenicians. If you drink it straightaway, it is spoiled and bitter. It must breathe. Let you think on this before we continue, then... When all is ready, speak and pray, tell us your personal truth that you may bless us with this wisdom."

Harkening his words, each became introspective and brooding. After some while Vuruk cleared his throat, stood, and began his tale.

"'Gold is reserved for they who heed the laws of gold.' And 'The sons of men are fools.'" Vuruk began. "These two ideas have been to me the most valuable birds inside of my mind. I have put them into use in the last five years, and yes, even the last ten while travelling with Kalabab. For I do indeed have a blessing to have been with him longer than you, and indeed have enjoyed it much. But as Faroud points out, to many this sounds like fortune has given me a better hand than the gods would allow. But it is not so. For I enjoy my work, and I believe this is my first lesson to share with you. That the work you do should make you happy. At least this lesson I learned with my own hands."

"So my tale begins not ten, but five years ago. Without jealousy I must now ask you to bear with my circumstances, for it was profitable for Kalabab to sell me his business."

Some booed him heartily but he waved them down.

"It was a bargain for me and it was shrewd of him. For he carried out his own loan against the business. I had to work doubly hard to pay him back but I did so in three years to own it outright. For two years now, I have been my own man. And in those two years, I have almost doubled the business I purchased. For my work makes me happy. Traveling all over this flat plane we dwell on, up north, south, and in all ways making coin. And though the raiding tribes have changed clothing and tactics and worship new gods, they all go down to the dirt when my spear pierces through them. I do indeed love this life, and would have it for no other. Begone oh useless chairs and tables. Give me an open road and my freedom!"

An uproar from the men, cheering the idea. As they were all long-voyage land traders, their thoughts echoed his own.

"But I did meet a man. A man of Edom, from a town near Petra. And I believe now, that I will tell him to you, for I did some business with him, and I believe it is the other most important thing that I learned from business with him. A lesson, not from around the campfire, but a lesson in blood. Now he was a common enough looking Samarian. Small, dark skinned with brilliant teeth. He proclaimed to have much wealth. And he loved to wear silver. I think he did cheat his own skin and my eyes by overlaying the silver on top of the pewter but that is for him to know only. But he adorned himself with almost his whole weight of the metal. Why, he even had a silver tooth in his mouth, he loved it so much. From every conceivable place stuck out and poked and banded this metal on his skin. It was like looking at a jeweler's cabinet to look at him. But in all his trappings, he had yet not much more coin in his purse than I, or so I believed. And maybe I believed less. But he talked as though we were equals.

At any rate, we were traveling from Ashkelon to Jerusalem, a small enough journey... When we were set upon by bandits in the hills. Now these were ordinary bandits, but our forces were small. I had sixteen men and he had but four. I had asked him to bring more but he swore that these four men were more capable than my own men, though they did not look it."

"They came at us with curved swords and ropes and all manner of devices to lay us down and rob us. But who did they attack from the onset? Was it me? Dressed like a humble worker in my rough spun tunic and robe? No! But my business partner firstly. They mowed through his four warriors like a dagger through sheep wool and tried to take my men on but were quickly routed. They did not take many animals, such was the venom from which my men fought, but they did take my partner. They drug him away and it was only after two days of searching that we did find him in a pit beaten and bloody. They had ripped off every ring from his body. He bled all over.

There were cuts about his neck from them sawing off his necklaces and his hands were worthless, for they cut the silver away from his fingers and wrists."

"His health was of my chief concern, for he was my partner! So we found a small village thereabouts and laid him up in the inn there. Being that he was too ill to travel, I paid the innkeeper five gold to tend after him and we would fetch him later when we finished our journey."

"Did he yet live?" asked Tartak.

"Alas no." Vuruk said solemnly. "For on our return from doing business in Jerusalem, we found him buried there in the hills away from the village. It plagued my conscience so that we were forced to return to Samaria to his family and give them his body, wrapped in the manner of the Edomites, and the coin from his sale. We had sold everything he had, including the animals, for we were undermanned to travel back again with so many. Upon our return, we realized that he had borrowed the animals from another trader and his family was forced to reckon with the sale of them. When we saw where he lived, it was but a hole in the ground and his family was destitute. The meager sum of coin remaining after all the debts were paid would not last them long. I gave them an alm from my earnings and went away hastily. I will never visit them again. But I will never forget the lesson."

"And what is this lesson that thou learned?" Kalabab asked.

"The more glimmer you have, the poorer you are." Vuruk said, and sat down.

"Such a wise lesson indeed," remarked Kalabab. "For in this lesson you did learn how much is given to the state of ones dress, only by the dogs that care for such things. And how also, how not much care is given by others who hold wealth in its true form. Gold should not be hung about ones neck. It should be busy in the hands of others, earning more gold for you. While I think thy mind is shrewd upon this subject, still, we all have much to learn from it. Who is next to tell their tale? How have you fared these last ten years with the wisdom so freely given to you?"

Richa Atad stood, his dark skin set aglow by the firelight. His long red and gray robes he gathered about him, and began his tale.

"I begin by simply stating that when I found myself on that very next morning ten years ago, with gold in my hand and the men about me setting off into town to go set themselves upon a large feast, a bit timid to their invitings. For I did not wish to spend all of my gold all at once. The third law of gold sang to me. 'Gold clings to the person who invests well.' Or so I remember it. So instead of following them into markets, I went to the stalls and found for myself one good donkey, some provisions, and went back home. On my way, I happened upon a caravan and they too were travelling in the same direction, so I fell in with them, and even had a little employment. My donkey carried me, but it was a strong beast so I also carried some goods for others."

"'Carry this small amount of salt for me and you may have some of it when we arrive.'" The caravan leader, Shuresh, told me. And so it was that upon our arrival, at Sela, he divvied up to me one twentieth of an ephah, for which I sold most at the market to one of the shopkeepers.

He also told me that they would be travelling to Tarsus straightaway. With barely enough time to kiss my mother and father farewell, I purchased two more donkeys for myself and all their tack so that I might carry more. Shuresh was quite pleased with my decision for the roads were more suitable to donkey than camel that farther north, and so he ascribed to me oils and precious spices, for of salt Tarsus had no need."

"This I did for one more year until my packs and men were equal to Shuresh. We had formed quite a bond between us, as well as my own friendship with his younger brother Suraam. It was the combination of these two men's advice that led me to my first largest rule. That you become in behavior like the people you listen to the most. Shuresh was a very wise man but Suraam was more amiable and pliable in willpower. Upon our parting ways, Suraam had decided that he would rather go with me on my journeys than with his brother. Shuresh was furious with him for this decision and it did not bode well with me to linger in Shuresh's company too long. Very quickly did we go on our way."

"Whatever bug had gotten into Suraam's mind about his quarrel with his brother festered and festered until, a month later, he was done with it. He stole two of my donkeys in mid journey and ran back to his brother. 'It is payment enough!' he cried as he sped away. What was I to do? Run him down and beat him? He was my friend and the brother to an even greater friend. I let him go, cursing the vault of the heavens overhead for my own misfortune and stupidity. For by listening to both men, had I become both wise and stupid at the same time... But in choosing to take the stupid man, I became all the more stupid."

"We have always known this!" Faroud shouted and the men laughed, to which Richa Atad kicked him soundly and he shut up. Richa Atad then continued.

"So! For those of you doubting my eventual wisdom," looking straight at Faroud as he said this, "It so happens that not four years later I caught up with Shuresh in Nisibis, north of Nineveh. He had been laid up two months or so with his brother, enjoying the town. It is not a large town, but as far as Shuresh tells it, they were no longer welcome in Nineveh. For Suraam's mind had not yet been set aright. He had taken to visiting the temple harlots that are so prevalent there. It seemed that this hobby of his ate up all of his time and his income. Now we all know that there are certain pleasures to be had by skillful women, but to devote yourself towards this as a lifetime pursuit was not in Shuresh's mind."

"Shuresh reasoned with him, talked to him, yea, even thrashed him soundly on the head once but Suraam would not harken to his brother's council. All of the gold that clinked into their purses, Suraam drained most quickly with offerings to the priestesses. To this day, I do not even know if Suraam worshiped these gods or did worship the thighs of the priestesses that served them."

"Please do tell us that thy second insight is from the thighs of priestesses!" shouted Vuruk. "For that is an insight I wish to have myself!"

Shouts arose from the men at this, but Kalabab shushed them down.

"But it is exactly that Vuruk," Richa Atad spoke solemnly, when they had all quieted down again. For the other insight I have learned most quickly from watching my old friend and his brother is this: 'Any hobby that does not serve to gain thy wealth, helps to deplete it.'" And with that, he sat down.

"Behold the soul of foolishness!" Vuruk said, scrambling to his feet. "Surely hobbies are there to be wasteful! Hobbies are there to ease the soul of troubles! This is the purpose of hobbies!"

"No" spoke Elipypes, another sly smile on his lips. "Hobbies are not leisure. Hobbies are a life pursuit of a thing. It does not matter what the thing is, but the pursuit of it is the hobby. It is true that a hobby may or may not help to gain wealth. For my father, who is now passed over, did have a hobby where he acquired some small amount of wealth."

"What was that?" Kalabab asked.

"He was a cloth weaver by trade. Sometimes during work, the spindles and loom pieces would break and be thrown away. He started collecting these small pieces and carving them with a little knife. He would make small delicate birds and figurines of the gods. Such was his detail that many people sought them. I say that he did not charge as much as he could have, for it was just a hobby, but he could have. And I think this is my contribution to the lessons tonight."

"But what is your story?" Kalabab asked inquisitively.

"I need not tell you my story," Elipypes countered. "I go here, buy that, move this, move that. I make money and my money makes money as the fourth law says I only invest in things that I am most familiar. But if you force me to add my own addition... My own lesson, it is simply this: 'Whatever your mind dwells on, your gold follows.' And it is as true as Richa Atad told us of his friend." And with that, Elipypes was quiet.

Kalabab stood, adjusted his pillow and sat back down.

"Are you up too late?" Vuruk asked.

"No." Kalabab said. "I was just looking around for more wisdom. But if the rest of you are as Elipypes, then I will go back to bed.

"Fine then. Faroud, you go next." Vuruk commanded.

"All I know is that I know nothing more than I already know." Faroud laughed.

All the others groaned the childish man.

"Tell us what you've learned or I will throw you in the fire!" Vuruk demanded.

"Fine, fine," Faroud sighed. "But I confess I am not priest or scribe nor lord to know such bleating. I work, I follow the 5 laws of gold, I give money to my sons for their businesses, and I continue. And..." He trailed off.

"And what?" Kalabab asked.

"And I am also becoming quite a wealthy money lender in Ecbatana." He smiled widely.

"Just as well," said Tartak. "With you owning all the money in the east, the rest of us are well to do in the other regions."

"Just so," Faroud smiled. "It happened quite by accident. I bought a large cave and some guards and now am quite wealthy. I've simply followed the five rules. I have them here." At this he stood up and took off his large blouse. On his waist was an overly large belt made of fine leather. On it sat five metal plates, and on those plates were carved the five rules.

Kalabab laughed long and hard. The others did as well, but Kalabab seemingly could not stop. His smile faded as he cried: "Oh, oh, oh! My sides! My sides!" Such was his merriment that it was causing great distress to him. When he eventually recovered, Faroud had sat back down and had clothed himself once again.

"Why do you laugh so?" asked Faroud. "It is not wisdom itself to carry with you the rules that bring you wealth?"

"Just so! Except that your compatriots have deemed themselves fierce enough to carve it upon their memory!" Kalabab cried, still laughing a little.

"Long have we known that his mind was not so fierce." Richa Atad said, smiling in jest but then turned serious. "But if he lives by the laws of the richest man in Babylon, who are we to disagree? For assuredly, though he does not look it, he may be the richest man here."

"Then let us make an adage for him." Kalabab decreed. "If he does not care to make one for himself, let us not waste this moment."

They all thought on this.

"That an ugly man is never helped by his clothes," said Vuruk.

"No, you dogs of the night. Lend to us thy brains! Let us reason this one into an actual form." Kalabab chided.

"Ah!" cried Tartak, "I have it. So. Let us suppose that all of us are killed by raiders tomorrow and all of the people Arkad ever talked to are also killed. The only remaining testament to this knowledge would be the belt yon cow-brains wears! So then Faroud is wiser than any of us give him credit to be. For without the preservation of knowledge, what your mind devises can be quickly stolen from you."

"Preserve knowledge so that it may not be taken away. Tartak has found the key to Faroud's lesson," said Kalabab.

They all reflected on the accidental proverb and each man thought of their businesses.

"It is a good lesson, Polcepias spoke up. Most of them had forgotten that he was there, so quiet was he. "For in the record keeping of wisdom there is but little. I know it is a custom still to smash a tablet of borrowing when it is repayed. To keep the tablet, to preserve it for eternity, this must only be used for the best of words. That being said, I would like to offer mine now."

"Indeed! For all others have had their turn!" Kalabab said. "Please regale us with your fine story."

"Well fine it is indeed but not for the speaker speaking it." Polcepias said. "For I do not speak much anywhere, even not to my five wives. But in action alone do I consider my best words."

He waited for the men to quiet, as there was some small glances at one another at the mention of his wives.

"When I was paid that night ten years ago, also like Richa Atad did I go into town, but not to cavort with the other men in the fine city. For the city was, and still is, wondrous to behold. But I did make my way to the Temple of Learning and stayed all day. I sought to understand the five rules that Faroud has so gloriously fashioned into a girdle. And so I stayed a week and then a month. I had very sparse lodgings and ate no expensive foods nor drank at all except the cheapest wine and water. And so there happened on me one day a large merchant. When I say large, I do mean it. For he was the fattest man I have ever seen. He was wearing all purple and gold and was from Kush or some part of the Upper Nile I do not know but his clothes were so majestic that when he spoke to me, all I could think about was the colorations thereupon. He offered me a job working in his dye-works, there in Babylon, for he had just recently started a business there. It was outside the gates of town and it included free lodging and two meals a day."

"Now he had taken me for a beggar and that is well and good, because I had sewn my gold into my rough belt, inside the lining. And so when I went to inquire as to the lodgings the head dye master welcomed me, for he had word of my arrival. I had no bags nor goods to move, so I stayed on and worked that day and the next."

"Hot barley and fish was on the larder every day and hard work all day. From sunup to sundown I learned how to crush the snails and sea-clams and churn them into color and how to render it down to slurry and how to make pastes and liquids and how to move the different cloths and how to dry them. There is not much more to it than that, but I craved every scrap of knowledge there was. I would do my job more quickly than all the others and then I would help my lord with other tasks not on my list. I became the hardest worker there."

"I was there for seven months in all when I had reached the pinnacle of my learning. The head dye master was sad to see me go because I had worked him out of his job those last months, doing all that he was doing so that he but rested most of the day. When I was paid by the Kushite man (again, I do not recall where he was from), I took a leisurely stroll around and throughout the city. I first visited one who gives baths and cuts hair and received a fine wash and cut along with a shave. Then I went to one who sells robes and received proper adornment."

"Now, mind you, I still had much of what we had earned from our trip here ten years ago, plus the paltry sum that I was paid by the dye master... It was almost exactly as much as I had spent. Now, when I had a goodly hair style and good clothes, I bought two bags, some shoes, a good walking stick, a few needed items for display, a few tablets, and hired a new servant to carry it all. But the bags were not empty long. For I then went to the east market and bought the best purple cloths and violet and periwinkle and other shades and hues that I had learned from my time in the dye-works."

"Being in such a specific industry, in such a small town, I knew when and where the buyers would appear and where to sell. Since I had bought at the east market where there was not much traffic, I went to the sellers' market on the other side of town. There were men who dealt in large numbers only and did not worry themselves with the smaller bolts that were sold to the seamstresses of the town to make clothes for fancy customers."

"It was then that I enacted my plan. For who knew that only hours ago I was but a peasant on the outskirts of town, mucking about in the dye-works. Not even my new servant knew this. For when I purchased him I was already bathed, shaved, and re-robed. Even though my hands may have had a bit of stain, this is expected of the merchants of purple. For that is what I appeared to be: a rich chief merchant."

The men nudged each other in the ribs and pointed at this. Polcepias continued, unfazed.

"I put my new turban on;it was purple and had a peacock feather in it. I had my servant set up a little easel to drape my newly acquired cloth on. For to the men in the market I had only brought a small sample of what I had available... Little did they know that I had spent every last copper on this gambit. I cried loudly as one does in the marketplace."

Polcepias leapt to his feet and began acting out his advertisement.

"Fresh Purple! The finest choices! Bolts on hand! Place your orders! No order too small!"

Boisterously yelling and dancing aboutPolcepias yelled and proclaimed. The men were startled at this dramatic change in the man. Yet just as soon as he had started, he smoothed his robes and sat back down. It was as if a peacock indeed had entered their midst, showed its feathers, squawked loudly and then returned to normal. When the men quieted, Polcepias continued in his normal state.

"This was my show-face. My entertainer side was unleashed – that which I had learned from watching the fat master in the markets. For I learned all the manners of making the clothes change color, but I also learned the business of the thing. For no one, recall, knew who I was or where I had come from. And they took the bait... Or the sale... and I had them on the hook. Order after order poured in that I had to send my servant to buy more tablets. And for a surety of the sale, I had them each pay one tenth of their order. No thought was given to their money, for I had purchased all the best goods and best shades from the market on the other side of town. They knew me not, but because of the demand, a false assumption of repute was adorned on me."

"I took my earnings that night to a gold-lender who knew me not. He was sore with me for the late hour but I pleaded with him to let me do business and he let me.Taking the money that I needed for the smallest merchants order, and setting it aside, I gave him the remainder as well as my sales samples. That night, my servant and I did not sleep much, though I know he must have been greatly fatigued, but he complained not for he was in my keep and I told him all would be well, come the morrow. We went to a tavern where he and I both ate a little and he slept at the table while I poured over my tablets doing the numbers."

"With the money I had created that day, I had enough to purchase the smallest merchants order, with only a small bit remaining. The profit from the first order would give me enough to fulfill the second-to-smallest order, and so on. Because I had taken all the sales on the same day, the only thing stopping me was the timing of the thing. If I could sell and buy and fulfil orders fast enough, I would do well."

"Early the next morning, before even the cocks had crowed, I aroused my servant and we went to purchase our first bolt. But the dye-works was closed still so I banged on the door until they let me in. I bought exactly what my order was, and not a copper more. I was shrewd in my dealings and no one there recognized me, for I had always been quiet and humble but when I was there, I was the loud self... The actor playing merchant; the ruse that must continue until this first round played out."

"All that day did I rush back and forth to the purple works, meeting my customers back at the largest market. A few of them must have thought me a madman. 'Why did he not bring everything at once?' they must have wondered. But besides the questions, it only served to deepen the mystery about this "New Purple Merchant," so they called me, for I did not ever give my name. That night, we had fulfilled five of the sales, but I had many more to go. Late in the evening, we found a clothing shop that had not yet closed and I got for him a turban like mine, also with a peacock feather, and a purple sash to wear on his chest. He liked it very much and his back stiffened with pride as he wore them. That night, we went to the same tavern and shared a room there together, and being exhausted, we were both fast asleep."

"In the morning we did it again. And the next day. And the next after that, working our way up the list from smallest to largest. After three days my servant had learned how to do the buying, so he was the one running to and fro - out of breath all day and not me. On the fourth day, we hired another servant, bought another turban and sash and carried on. By weeks end we only had one customer who was not fulfilled but I did not need him. I appologized profusely to him, gave him back his surety with interest, and moved our shop to Borsippa, not far south from here. I have done this and similar for the last ten years."

"You have made fortunes selling only purple died cloth?" Kalabab probed.

Polcepias smiled, knowingly. "Not just. For not two years into it did I become tired of buying from others. I acquired ships and fleets and caravans and a dye-works. I did not seek to control much of the purple cloth industry, for I sought to control the whole of the purple industry."

The men were quiet, amazed at the brilliance of the man.

"Too much coin flowed from my hands to the snail harvesters, to the mills, to the weavers, to the cloth transporters. I said to myself: If I controlled it, all the money would stay in my grasp. And so it has. And knowing what I do now of both purple and of caravans, I achieved what I sought. Taking the purple industry from the sheep and snail to the party-room of the rich. For the rich do not want to lend a hand in the creation of an object, they expect to purchase a product and be done with it. For their gold speaks for themselves.

So by buying the sheep, buying the farm, buying the harvesters, buying the transporters, the loomers, and all steps in between, I controlled all of the market from start to finish. As a matter of fact, when one part of the process does well, we sell that product on the market. Excess wool? Sell it at the market. Excess caravan workers? Hire them out. Excess dye? Sell it to the weavers. There is not a part of the process that could not do well on its own. I make money while saving money at the same time." Polcepias smiled widely, much pleased with his own wisdom. But in all my getting of wealth, I will now come to the one thing that I have learned aside from the five laws of gold."

"There was a moment, two years ago, when I was buying some small fleet on Cyprus, that I came across a woman and her family. She scolded me for the purchase of the fleet. I asked her why her scorn was directed to me? I was bringing in good work and good money to her town. And I shall never forget her words to me, for they stung like the barb of a scorpion."

"You do rob from the individual to feed your greedy enterprise." She said.

"At first I did not understand what she meant, but I have learned that she is right. To completely control a thing means that you cannot grow that thing. Demand grows on goodwill, not on greed. For marketability is based on the desire of the consumer. So, the opposite reaction is strangely, the truest one. You encourage growth when you feed your competition."

All were quiet, waiting for him to finish. He paused, letting his words sink in.

"Think on it. If at the market, they all decided to go home, and you had to go to each of their houses to buy their goods, what pleasure would that bring? It would only serve to disgruntle the consumer of their goods. But, bring in all the pearl merchants to one place and suddenly, like a horde of locust, all the customers will buy and buy and buy them up. Think about when you walk down the food stalls. Do not all the stalls help the others? Yes, in some cases a single stall does well by itself, but it is a novelty at best. The best food stalls all cram in next to each other stemming from this same idea. The customer will come. The customer always comes. For they know that now they can save time and buy many foods all in one place. Again I tell you: you encourage growth when you feed the competition."

"The woman that I told you about has a family and they have one small vessel that they hunt the snails and sea life to make purple dye. Were I to take that away, how could I compete with her and she with me? But it is because she is allowed to operate outside of my domain that she and I will both prosper. Think of this: What if, in all her desire to create wealth, one of her sons creates a quicker way to make dye? Some new learning? Will that help us both out eventually? Yes. For I assure you, someone will do to me what I did to my fat master so long ago."

"Stealing!" Cried Vuruk.

"Borrowing," clarified Polcepias. "Think on it! Who taught Kalabab the five rules of gold?"

"Nomasir!" Tartak said.

"And who taught Nomasir?" Polcepias asked.

"Arkad." Faroud said.

"But then, who taught us?" Polcepias asked, yet again.

"I did!" Kalabab laughed. He understood the point Polcepias was driving home.

"So then, who is the thief? Am I a thief? Is Nomasir? Is our former master Kalabab? I declare that we are either all thieves or we are all wise men. And I for one, am no thief."

The fire popped as the last of the embers were dying. It was cold and the rest of the camp had already returned to their tents. All the men gazed into the fire, lost in their own thoughts. Eventually Elipypes broke the silence.

"Polcepias, is this your first time back to Babylon, ere since you left so long ago?"

"Yes." Polcepias said, gazing back at him and then back to the fire. "I mean to visit a man."

"Whom wilt thou visit?" Kalabab asked.

"The man who I let borrow my gold." Polcepias answered.

"What?" Richa Atad asked. "Who is this you speak of?"

Polcepias laughed. "Do you not recall the beginning of my story? The gold lender!"

"What?" Vuruk yelled. "You mean he has had your gold these long years?

"Yes." Polcepias said. "And if my numbers are correct, I should be able to collect 1,000 pieces."

3

Kobbi the Musician

Little is known of Bansir's friend Kobbi, we know only of his life through the tale of his friend. But his tale is not without merit, for in the absence of Bansir, after he had moved to Nineveh, Kobbi's life began to take on a new meaning. For though Kobbi was outgoing and friendly with all that were about him, his goals of owning a large lyre and a school to teach all was largely fulfilled. His three sons and two daughters each were happy and his wife was content and the master of her household. Even though Kobbi had known his new wife only known her for 8 years, their five young children were her joy and song.

From time to time, Kobbi would find himself at the temple of learning, and there be involved with the discussions of the merchants of Babylon who frequented the place. Though not ever invited to attend the lessons of Arkad, he had heard of the seven cures to a lean purse.

Pay yourself first, control thy expenditures, make thy gold multiply, guard thy treasure from loss, make your home a profitable investment, insure future income, and increase thy ability to earn. These seven lessons were well and good, but Kobbi never put together how to have it apply to his own life, until well after Bansir had left him for Nineveh. Surly from time to time, he would stop over at the old workshop and talk with Nahmbir, Bansir's oldest son… But it was not the same. The son was not the father, and though he enjoyed the boys company, it was not the same.

So Kobbi began more and more to go to the Temple of Learning and listen in on the conversations. He made a pledge to himself, as he often did in these situations where he found himself out of his depth. "Oh Kobbi," he said to his soul, "Listen well and learn what these wise men have to say to you." And so it was that he did. Long had he known that good cheer and skilled music could earn him much coin, but his desires started growing deeper than that. Much coin was good, but what if an accident should befall him? What if he lost his voice due to some horrible calamity? What would happen then if he could not sing and play nor train his students to sing and play? What good would he be if he could not earn? His passion for this possibility drove him into a frenzy of fear. He must ensure for his wife and children that this would never happen.

"Good luck can be enticed by accepting opportunity." One man stated. This was new to Kobbi. He addressed the man who had said it.

"Good sir, I confess that I have not encountered this phrase before. It is one of great interest to me. How did you come by it?" asked Kobbi.

"Why it is from The Richest Man in Babylon." The man said, puffing his chest. "He gives to us his wisdom and we translate it for him."

"Oh he most certainly does not let us translate it…" another man began, "For he asks us all to translate it ourselves."

"Yes!" said a third man, approaching them. "The Richest Man in Babylon asks questions of us, and lets us discuss for ourselves what the outcome of that question is. It is only at the end of the discussion that he gives us his opinions of it."

"I understand now." Kobbi acquiesced, bowing to the men. He was not wise like they were - these merchants of so much wealth. Who was he to even ask questions?

"But wait a moment," the second man said. "You are the friend of Bansir, the chariot builder? And are you not also a friend of The Richest Man in Babylon?"

"At my heart, I only know him as Arkad, for we were childhood friends, and yes, also Bansir. We went to Temple together and played as youths. But I must be honest, I was not invited to the original learning group of one hundred men, so from then until now I have stayed away, plying my trade and teaching my disciples."

"But all men are free to come discuss things the mind desires," the first man said. "It is here that we find more knowledge and learning, even though our Great King Sargon is at his new Palace, still the leaning continues."

"And you are Kobbi, the musician. Surely your great songs come from such a places as wisdom? Or do you pluck your lyrics from the dark abyss of dreams? Or perchance they come from the gods themselves; surely I have heard you play and there is no sweeter sound in all of Babylon than your lips and fingers."

Kobbi bowed low. "It is indeed kind of you to say, and again very much so, unsolicited. For usually men say such things only as they are giving me coin after I have wooed it out of their pockets with the sweet twangings of my instrument."

The men laughed good-naturedly at this and Kobbi took his leave. "Good luck can be enticed by accepting opportunity." He repeated to himself, and so, he journeyed home.

The next morning, his wife found him alone on the porch, stroking his beard. His azullu pipe in one hand, and with the other hand, he held a small bone drum. The blue smoke from his pipe lay in lazy coils around him, the air moist and still from the night. He looked as though he were deep in thought so left him there until after she had woken the rest of the household. When she returned, he was in the same position, though the bowl of the azullu pipe was empty. He was banging a slow beat on the drum. When she appeared he looked at her.

"You had best be up and away upon my return." She told him sternly.

"I have done that already." He replied.

"And you lie to your wife like as in one of your fancy tales my husband. Do not do me like this." She huffed.

"Ah! My dearest dove! No, come back! I have already been out and away. The school is tended, I have no appointments, and I am deep in thought on how to acquire an easier life for you." He smiled that Kobbi smiled and her heart melted, as it always did.

"Dearest singer of songs," she began, more softly, "what schemes do you scheme this day?"

"Last night I pondered and pondered upon my walk home. And so much was my pondering that indeed I walked well into morning. I stopped by the house of Jarakad Nada, my chief assistant, and aroused him from his slumber. I instructed him what to do in school today, and arranged for him to take the whole of the school under his wing for the afternoon. Thereafter I returned here, filled my pipe and smoked it. After this, you appeared."

"Well such as it may be, thou thinkest that I do not see laziness when I see it," she said.

"Not laziness dearest cucumber. For I only seek to understand that which I have learned last night at the Temple of Learning." Kobbi pleaded.

"And what is that?" She asked.

"That good luck may only be found when one has the deep longing to engage in opportunity. And such I believe that I have a plan to do so." Kobbi smiled at her, his famous smile. "I shall tell you of my plan when it becomes as stone within my mind, for right now, it is still a river. Soon it will be mud, and then it shall be stone."

"Husband of mine, I do not know if that is how stones are formed but I shall give thee thy space in thine head to do such ruminations until I see thee again, after I go to market. Thy sons and daughters cry for thee even as thou sit at this moment. See to them. Become a father as well as a thinker of deep things. Good bye." She said, grabbing her purse and her small basket, and walked out the front gate, not giving her eloquent husband time to respond.

And thus, it was later that morning that she returned to find herself under the onslaught of a cacophony coming from within the house. Upon entering, laden with leeks and pears and grains and carrots, she found her whole household in a circle on the floor, each with an instrument in hand. The younger ones had small drums, and it was these that gave most of the audible discomfort.

"Are you trying to rouse the dead from their graves?!" She shrieked when she came inside. All sound ceased at the scene of the angry mother. Children scrambled away, seeking the comfort of their own beds and away from the furious woman who had given them birth.

"Not so, not so dearest rabbit! For I have come up with a plan to enrich the sounds of one instrument by adding a second, third, and a fourth! And I plan to practice this technique on the morrow at my school! Many times I have steered students away from the school were they not proficient in singing or on the lyre. But by adding the lute, the woodwind and the drums, we see that it does not matter. Skill versus skill alone, the drum may not be the most beautiful of instruments, but when joined in unison with a string, it is a wonder! I have seen others do this, but only from the highly decorated priests. I never had the gall or the impudence to think that I also might join this style of my own, much less teach it to my students. For I believe that this idea that sloshed so freely about in my mind has born much fruit. I plan to go to the school now and enact my strategy."

She stood there, her groceries in her hand, thinking that he was either the most foolish musician to ever have walked the earth, or the brightest. Only time would tell.

And so it was that Kobbi was right, for his school saw much increase, and many students had to be turned away. Jarakad Nada as it turned out was a very excellent wood-wind and drum player and often he and Kobbi would be sought to play for audiences here and there, in the houses of the rich. His school increased to two schools, one on each side of Babylon. His wife and children helped, taking turns teaching classes or tending to the books, and life was good to them for a brief while.

But fortune, unguarded, may cause great distress when least expected. For two things happened at once in Kobbi's life that left him doubting all he had done. Firstly, Jarakad Nada had rebelled against Kobbi and started his own school. There was no way for Kobbi to be in two places at once, and so Kobbi was forced to resign the other school to Jarakad Nada for a small sum. The second thing that happened was beyond bad luck, for not two nights after resigning the second school, the first school burned. There was great speculation as to how it happened, but, for whatever reason that it did, it almost ruined Kobbi. Each and every instrument that he had owned, save one small lyre, had been burned in the fire and was beyond repair. That not being the end of things, inside of the building was so damaged by fire and smoke that the building was unusable and there was no other place to hold school except for a certain cow pasture, on the outside of town. The owner of the pasture had one of the students in the school and he gladly lent them the land. It didn't take much thinking to know that many of the parents and the students themselves did not want to stand around in a cow pasture. Thus, Kobbi was forced to take a loan to find a new building, but fortune's cruel sword was harsh and he could not recover enough students in time to pay rent and the loan both and eventually had to close the doors altogether... Now, deeply in debt.

And here he was, plying his trade on the market corners, like he had done years before. Yes, here was the great Kobbi, teacher and mentor to hundreds of youth, stripped of all he had invested. He mourned for himself, trying the pity play on the streets, making it known how miserable his state had become, but not one copper did he receive in payment from the crowds. For in his line of work, the sad song was a rare one and must be accompanied by many happy songs around it. No one wanted to see a sad musician on the streets. So he played the happy ones and made some coin. Just enough to play certain men to keep away from his belongings, for his debt was increasing daily; enough to give to the wife for the household needs, assuredly, for clothing and curds were not free. He could ask Bansir's son for a loan, but such was his pride that he did not even consider it.

But he was not idle. No not Kobbi, after all he had learned. When he was singing, or taking a break from singing, he was devising his new rules to live by. He had created them based upon his woes, and what he had learned from them. Modeled after Arkad's Seven Cures for a Lean Purse, he called them: "The Seven Tablets of

Earning." But were they foolish or were they words to live by? He had been so unfortunate at this late stage in his life that he could not afford to make mistakes with the rest of it. Here he was, almost an old man, still learning how to start. He must know. He must! The only way to find out if they were of any merit was to present them to the Temple of Learning. For it was the one place where the men of money gathered to speak openly about such things. He would go there and present his ideas to them. He did so that very night.

The sun was still hot and Kobbi had only taken a small break for food and water once in the heat of the day. He was famished but the few coins in his wallet were already spoken for. He stopped outside the Temple of Learning – so grand a building it was, and listened in. Many voices, and yes, the voice of Arkad rumbled on about this or about that. He did not want to go in, but go in he must, for if he was walking down a road that led to ruin, he needed these men to tell him so. The room was in mid-discussion.

"…and I feel that were I to buy this parcel of land off of the owner, then I would never be able to get my camels to it, for the journey is long. This is why I've refused. I believe it to be in my best interest." Said a tall thin dark man with a shaven face. His green robes and hat meant that he was probably from Meshech. Such a long way to travel. But then again, Arkad was very famous and people did come very far to listen to him, even as they had to Solomon, so many years ago.

"Very sound, very sound indeed." Said Arkad from his small platform. Are there any other men here who have found new successes or new ideas?" He mused. A woman stood up. Dressed in the attire of the Aksumites, of the upper Nile.

"Though I am not a man, am I permitted to speak, or do I require a phallus to enter debate? Pray tell me it is not so, for there are many a eunuch here today who have spoken their minds."

Laughter erupted from the room as Arkad's hand waved them down.

"Nay, nay my good woman, for this is a Temple of Learning, and all are welcome from the King to the lowest slave. I pray thee, speak on. What wisdom would you like to tell us?"

"Only this. That in my country there are many who perform the arts for the rich and the poor alike and are met with high reverence. Yet today, as I was wandering about your fair city I saw but one man, singing and playing a sad lyre that was not fit for a pauper. By the looks of him, one might say that he had seen good times but the gods must have spit him out of their mouth. I ask thee and this great company of people… How are the arts supposed to flourish without the support of the people? Where is the gaiety and mirth that should frequent such a place? And how is it that the ones who bring us these songs and tales go hungry? That is all." And with that, she sat down.

"That is Kobbi!" A man from the side called. "Sad is his tale!"

"Kobbi it is indeed." Arkad said, as he stood. "And as the gods have it, it is the man himself who has just walked into our presence." He gestured to Kobbi and all eyes turned to him. "Come Kobbi. Tell us your tale so that we may all learn. For fortune has indeed smiled upon us that you arrived just now."

Never in his life had Kobbi been embarrassed to perform. But never in his life had Kobbi ever been under these circumstances. He slowly made his way to the front, passed the oiled and perfumed merchants, passed the robed traders, passed several men who he knew their first name. He stood at the front of the room and set his lyre down.

"Might I ask for a glass of water, or wine perchance before I begin my tale?" He asked sheepishly.

Someone on the front row quickly gave him a goblet. He slaked his throat and began his tale.

Now we who read this already know his tale, for it is a sad one, and so when he was finished telling it to them in this story, they were greatly disheartened and mourned with him.

"Never should it come to this!" cried one man.

"Alas poor Kobbi" cried another.

The Aksumite woman wept openly.

Arkad quieted them, one by one.

"Few have the bravery to share with us this tale so fresh as an open wound. Yet there must be province in it, for he to arrive just as this so bold a woman ask about him. Pray Kobbi. Tell us what you know. What is the wisdom that you have gleaned so far? How may other men find caution in your tale?"

Kobbi looked at him with a dazed expression. "Truly it is providence indeed for me to be here just now, in just such a way. For today I have found the wisdom enough to come by my own set of rules to live by. Similar in temperament to your seven cures, I am sure, but maybe not so much full of wisdom? That was the true intent of my journey here tonight after plying my songs on the corner."

"Say on!" Sang out Aksumite woman.

"Indeed!" Said Arkad. "Tell us all!" and sat down.

"In my wanderings since the great calamity that overcame me, I've come upon what I feel are seven key understandings to open up the mind to how and when your life may be directed. It is all about the people you know and the people who have power over you, or the people you have power over. I will share these with you now in list, for I have not yet put it to song."

There was a light smattering of laughter and Kobbi started.

"Rule the first: Know who holds the vault-stone. By understanding the debt of a thing, you may understand how to best keep out from under it. Is there usury or is it a rental? By knowing who holds the key to the vault, you may incur good debt... Debt that is not insurmountable. For in procuring bad debt, you bury yourself alive."

"Rule the second: Know who holds the purse-string. By understanding who controls a store, or a family, or a company of people you begin to learn how to approach that group with a keen understanding. If you ply your wares in front of the wrong person, then you reap not a reward."

"Rule the third: Know who holds the dagger. By understanding that person that can hurt you, you are able to seek safety from them. If you do not know who your enemies are, then how can you protect yourself? By understanding your competitors and your foes, then you may learn how to better your safety."

"Rule the fourth: Know who holds the chariot reigns. By understanding the law and the effects of the law, you can directly find the correlations between new edicts and your business. Will it be legal to sell bread by the Temple during a holiday? If it is or if it is not is of utmost importance. The more knowledge you have, the safer you are."

"Rule the fifth: Know who holds the counting stones. By understanding where all of your money is, where all of your interest lies, by knowing how the affairs of your purse is, will guarantee that you do not over budget for delights and non-essential items. Will this donkey be a hindrance of a benefit? If you cannot control how much flows out of your purse, then fate will decide for you."

"Rule the sixth: Know who holds the keys. By understanding who the person is who can open the right door, you will be able to go through doors other cannot by force alone. For any door can be broken, but when the robber is outside, the soldiers are called to arrest him. But by knowing the key-holder, you walk right in."

"Rule the seventh: Know who holds the tablets: By understanding the men who know the scores to all the games you are able to understand where to best strike next. Does a man owe another man so much that he cannot pay it and will lose his goods? How will that affect you? Opportunities are unlimited when you know those who write everything down. The record-keeper, many times, is king."

The long tapered oil candles sputtered and sparked as condensation was drawn up into them by the cooling night. The room lay still. Outside, the sun had set and the sounds of the city were dying down. The hall lay in a hushed quiet, deeper than if it had been empty.

Slowly, and without provocation, the men in the room stood and came up to the platform. Some grasped his hands and some bowed. But all of them, one by one placed a gold or a silver into Kobbi's small purse that he had placed down by his lyre. There was a reverence to the hall, and a great many men cried as they made their way to the front. Then, standing before him was Jarakad Nada.

"I am sorry you had a fire my master," Jarakad Nada said. "Know that it was not I that set the fire, but please accept my gift as a token of my appreciation for you and for my attitude being that of a prodigal. Tomorrow morning, I will send one half of my students and instruments to you. You will have a school once again. Where one of us prospers, we may both prosper." Jarakad Nada's tears spilled down his tunic and he hugged Kobbi tight."

"But where am I to hold school?" Kobbi wondered aloud.

"In the new hall that I will build for you," said Arkad. "Also, will I erase your debt. You can pay me a small sum until the whole amount is paid off. I charge no interest and you have until we both die to repay."

Kobbi was speechless.

"Only for a small price do I require these things," Arkad continued. "I am old and do not know if I will see the fruits of my labor with you. So I ask you that your Seven Tablets of Earning be added to the Wisdom of the thoughts from this great hall. Work on the tablets has already begun. I only ask that you say 'yes.'"

And so it was on this very night, that The Seven Tablets of Earning were placed into record as part of the collection of the Chronicles of the Wisdom of Gold. Kobbi's fortune grew that night in unforeseen ways as well, for Arkad's building was made in such a way that the music simply soared through the air. Besides the twelve Jarakad Nada sent over from his school, Kobbi's first two students were the two daughters of the Aksumite woman.

4

Rodon the Spear Maker

Fifty pieces of gold! Only once before had Rodon, the spear maker of Babylon carried so much in his wallet. Happily down the street he strode. Never before had he done business so quickly than this, except for the first fifty that he had made, not ten years ago. He would add it to the collection at Tryphon's Gold Exchangery, where he had met Tryphon's father, on that grateful day that had begun his success. He had interrupted Tryphon's father, Mathon during his meal, but that had not mattered. Mathon had graciously accepted Rodon and tackled his problem head on.

Arriving at his store, he announced himself: "Behold Tryphon, I am come to see thee, that thou might exchange for me this heavy bag about my waist!" Rodon did not fear that anyone else overheard him, for he was a large man, and in the prime of his adulthood. Plus the armored Warrior at the door was a rough looking man. All day long he stood there, at the ready, should someone try to steal from Tryphon.

A scuttling and shuffling and a loud clanking were heard from the inside of the shop. "Come inside Rodon! For I confess that I do not want to go out in the sun to greet you, for my eyes hurt and do water much when I go out!" Tryphon yelled out to him, from inside the dim shop. With an eye and a nod to the guard, Rodon went inside the shop. There were no windows open to the outside, only the front door let in a little light from the ox skin that hung over the front door. It was so dark that lanterns had been set up and the whole place smelt of oil and tallow.

"Thou needest to open up thine eyes to the greater world about thee," Rodon stated, as his eyes adjusted to the gloom. "You are sitting in the dark while the rest of the day goes on about its business! And also, have you thought about my proposal? Do you wish to sell? For I confess I am making more and more gold every day but my arms grow more and more heavy. I would hear an answer!" Rodon's eyes finally found Tryphon in the corner, hunched over a box. He was having problems lifting it.

"Ehh!" Tryphon called, as he struggled to lift the box. "Rodon, come here and lift this box and set it upon this stool here. For it is too heavy for my old bones."

Rodon came over, lifted the box to the table and was about to set it down, when Tryphon squealed. "Not yet!" and grabbed a tablet from off the table. "Now." He said, and Rodon set it down. As he was setting it down, Rodon recognized it straightway. It was Mathon's old token chest!

"I did not know you had this still!" Rodon said, as he gazed at it. "It is but the very same chest that I did gaze upon not ten years ago." Rodon's gleaming teeth were set in an almost perpetual smile as he remembered it.

"And yet it is just as heavy and cumbersome." Tryphon whined.

"Bah!" Rodon said. "It is not heavy at all!"

"For a man such as you who toils over the bronze caster, maybe," said Tryphon. "But for an old man such as me, it is a chore to lift."

Rodon burst out into a loud laugh. "You are younger than I!" He proclaimed. "You are even younger than my wife. Not even twenty winters are you old!"

Tryphon grimaced at this. "And yet I age more quickly than most, I profess. It is but the weight of gold upon my years that does speed the years by so quickly. I daresay were someone to relive me of this burden, I would most quickly accept."

Rodon thought on this, for maybe the gods did tell him something even right now. "Tryphon. I have known thee most of thy adult life. When your father left us for the darkness that lay below our feet, did I know thee even then. You knew what fortune had in store for me and the blessings I would endure, much as your own blessings. Yet we have both succeeded. We have both taken wives of good humor and are easy to look upon... Yet now as I was walking here today I was asking whatever shall I do with my amassing fortune. And now, even right now, you ask if there is someone to take over for you? I must confess that I know just as much as you about gold-lending... For not only do I own my own workshops and trade in metal, but I too have done much lending. Come. Were you to sell your business, how much would you ask of it, were I asking right now?"

Tryphon was unnerved. For though he complained much, he had never given it serious consideration. He did not think that anyone with their wits about them would like to have bought his business. He sat down on the floor and asked in earnestness: "Thou art playing a jest on me? Doest thou ask in all earnestness this question? That you wish to buy my business? How can I tally a price?" He spread his arms wide. "That all you see is mine and my effects both personal and business are strewn about me."

Rodon squinted. "Then I shall ask a price for all you have. That you may be able to take your gold and pack lightly. That I would set you up with a goodly sum that thou might retire from this line of work and do what you please. That you take what you want, and sell me the rest."

"A bargain this would be had I not my wife and two daughters to consult." Tryphon said.

"Then do so now," Rodon said. "I shall wait." He smiled again.

So Tryphon went out the side to the adjoining small house, where his family dwelt. Rodon thought about the wisp of a man who had inherited his father's business. Mathon had left it all to him after his death. Indeed, even while Mathon was still alive, Tryphon helped him in the shop. Their slaves, earners themselves, had bought their freedom, such was the wisdom of Mathon to those who worked under him. A wise lender and a better steward of his own household. Ando, the slave and his wife and his son, upon purchasing their freedom had volunteered to serve as workers for Mathon even then. For the slave debt had been paid, and Mathon was a just man. Large Bartha, Ando's son, was the gate keeper to the shop. He had no military training, but was an able warrior and good guard, all the same. Old Ando served in the same capacity at night, and his wife, Jusamana helped clean the workshop and the house. In this, they earned their keep and stayed in the small quarters on the property, in a smaller house.

Rodon looked around at the mess. Tablets strewn here and there among eating utensils, clothes, and various wares were piled on one another in a reckless way. The windows that used to let in the day were mortared up with cob and brick. Lamps hung here and there to give the place an unnatural dim gloom. What a wreck it had become, a far cry from Mathon's house of yesterday.

Tryphon emerged with his wife from the door.

"She thinks you rob me." He said. "Tell her the truth."

Rodon smiled at his small wife. She was not as beautiful as the last time he saw her. For in living with the son of his friend, she had become miserly herself, not only in deed, but in makeup. Wrinkles around her eyes and her bent stature showed her double the age that she had been when Tryphon and she had wed.

"My good lady," Rodon began. "I have in my leather wallet here" he said, drawing out the wallet from his belt, "fifty gold pieces. By chance it was ten years ago that I walked into this very room with my first fifty pieces and the father of your husband showed me best how to use it. Since that day, I have prospered where no other man has prospered as a bronze smith, a silver smith and a gold smith. A trader and lender also have I become, as you know. I have done business with your husband continually and even now seek to do business with him in a just manner. You have always known me for a good man and a good man I remain."

He set the wallet down on the table, loosed the strings, and pouring out the gold upon it. "Here is a small dowry upon thy business, and let us call it that. For just as a man gives to the groom an amount for the hand of his daughter, so it must be here. Does not the code of Hammurabi speak of this? Can we even consider it in such a fashion or do we speak to each other as customers do speak at the market without friendship or bond? For you know how fondly I am with you and with your family, and the children of our hands are our businesses... So I seek to marry yours to mine. I will give you and your husband the freedom you so earnestly seek, and you will remand to me the heartache that has become this enterprise. No longer will you have to worry and fret about this sale or that loan... You will be free and may do what you please. For know this: I will pay you not one year but ten years' worth of reward for this business. And this fifty gold is simply a gift, left on the table from an old friend for you hearing him." So saying, Rodon sat down.

She looked Rodon up and down, then looked about the room, and then finally her husband. "Do what thou wilt. Perhaps it may be best to sell all and move, for my mind is numb and my heart is weary being in this house all the day. Let us raise our children where the grass is greener, away from the shadow of your father." She said, and went back through the door.

Tryphon sat down on the floor again, his hands in his lap. Rodon could tell his mind was racing with the possibilities of the sale.

"Ten years worth?" He asked Rodon.

"As I have said." Rodon answered.

Tryphon's hands went absentmindedly to the token box and held its side. With a thought, he opened it. "Remember these?" He asked Rodon.

Of the tokens, Rodon remembers every one, for attention to small details and lists was always part of his life. The bronze neck piece and scarlet cloth: The man who loved a woman to his poverty and her funeral arrangements. For she had killed him and then herself. The borrowers were dead and they had no relatives to repay. These two tokens still remained in the token box, and, on top of it... Such was the lesson that Mathon had learned for himself. The ox bone ring had come and gone in and out of the token box many times but had ceased two years ago when they no longer decided to take out loans, for they were doing so well. Ah, it was not here anymore but the rare gold bracelet with carvings from Sumer. That had been sold to a priest of the moon god, for a profit against the loan that would never be repaid. The loan was forgiven, although that fat old hag was furious with me.

Having never wanted to repeat the lesson, the turquoise scarab had been sewn to the top of the inside of the box, next to the words: "Better a little caution than a great regret"

Rodon knew that he would never see Nebatur's single knotted rope again, but there were some like it. One knot meant one herd; two knots meant two, and so on. Nebatur had died around three years ago, but fortunately, he did not have a loan out at the time, so there was no knotted rope here.

"I remember every one. Though there are new ones here that I do not know." Rodon answered. For there were ten more that he could see among the other tokens, and knew them not.

"This is the old way of doing things. My father's way. I still employ those methods from time to time, but I thought more money would be made in the trading of one gold to the next. A Nineveh gold to a Babylon gold. Each mint with its own measure, and that I would collect the small allowance from each trade. Business is small but what customers I do have I earn less than I thought. For they can just as easily trade in the marketplace on their own accord. Of the tokens you do not recognize, they are loans that cannot or will not be repaid. I confess if it were not for my father's old customers, I would have no profitable business at all. And my money escapes me in other ways. For Ando and his family do not pay for their house a rent, and I do pay them much more than they deserve, for their friendship with my father hangs over my head like a cloud." He sighed and ceased speaking.

"They do not pay a rent?" Rodon asked, raising his eyebrows.

"Nay. For I have the obligation to pay for them all I make, for they were slaves." Tryphon answered.
"But they are freed now." Rodon asked. "So why do you not treat them like the free men they are? Why give them favor where no favor is earned? Do they not provide services for you that you pay them regularly?"

"Ah yes. But it is to curry favor with the gods and fortune that I pay them double their earnings and charge them not rent." Tryphon said.

Rodon's face darkened but he said nothing. After he was calm he stood and dusted off his robe. "Tell me your decision in the morning. Arrange a price and I shall give it to you." Rodon said. And with that, he walked out the shop, nodded to Bartha, and went home.

Rodon's family and servants were there on his return. Later in the night when the city had quieted, Rodon went to the rooftop on his house to think. The house had been built by an Israelite craftsman and had the balusters set around it as was their fashion. Rodon, sitting on a small camp chair, put his feet up on the top railing, and began to eat some sugared figs. This was his habit when he had a large problem in front of him that he did not know the answer to. His wife found him there, and stood beside him.

"I knew that when I found the figs missing, I would find you here." She said. "What troubles your heart?"

"Your father was a slave, was he not?" He asked, looking up at her. Being the wife of a rich man, she could afford to adorn herself with paint on her eyes in the manner of the Egyptians. Her eyes shown brightly though the blue, black, and green of the paint.

"A long while ago, at one of the many ziggurats of Ur, he was a bricklayer." She began. "He worked hard and saved until he bought his way out of slavery." She looked down at him. "Why? Are you trying to save enough to buy your way away from me?"

They both laughed at this. "My dear woman. I would pay everything I had and more just to be able to marry thee again." He pulled her onto his lap, kissed her, picked her up and got off the chair. Setting her down he kissed her again and motioned that they should stand together. "Look there. What do you see?" He asked.

"The camel stables?" She asked.

"No out passed our courtyard. Five streets up." He pointed.

"Oh? Is that the house of your old friend Mathon? His son's business now?" She ventured.

"By the gods, what a mind you have!" He proclaimed. "Yes. The very same man. I have told him that I would buy his business today. Tomorrow I will find out his reply."

"Is it profitable?" She asked.

"It could be. But Mathon's son drives away good business with foolish ideas. Were he to embrace wisdom, he would profit. But he does not the things that I have learned to make money.

"Ah!" She wriggled out of his grasp and threw her arms wide, as if to embrace the sky. "The Laws of the Flow of Wealth! By the ever wise Rodon!"

He grabbed her again, bent her over and kissed her hard. "I will show thee ever wise." And took her to their bedroom.

The next morning, Rodon was at Tryphon's house early enough to see Ando, sitting by the gate He was the same man that he had known for these last ten years, but he was older.

"Not standing guard?" Rodon asked.

"If thieves may come I can see them well enough from here." Ando said.

"That is true enough. Tell me, does Tryphon suffer much from bandits? Has there been trouble in the past?" Rodon asked.

"No, there have never been bandits... Though the way Tryphon tells it, all men desire to rob him. His idea is to make sure that there never is any bandits by having my presence always here, or my sons, during the day." Ando answered.

"Yet Mathon never had bandits." Rodon said.

"Mathon was maybe wiser. He treated everyone with friendship instead of suspicion." Ando answered. Bartha then came out of the door. Surprised to see Rodon, he eyed him up and down, he then looked at his father. "Mother seeks thee."

Ando got up and saluted Rodon. "May the gods shine upon thee." He said, and went inside.

Rodon watched as Bartha set up his post from the way his father had arranged it. "Your father was telling me of all the bandits that do try and rob you." Rodon asked. Bartha furrowed his brow. "There are no bandits. They do not come. I am here." He stood firmly. "No bandits... Just me."

Rodon nodded, realizing that he could not compete with that wisdom. "Very good. I venture to ask if your master is ready for the day? May I go inside?"

"Yes. When I am outside, Tryphon is inside." He said, looking forward instead of at Rodon.

Rodon lifted the skin and started to go in when Bartha interrupted. "I am so sorry, but... Before you visit with my master, might I ask of you but one question?" Rodon lowered the skin and turned. "Yes my friend of a friend, what might that be?"

"You are Rodon the spear maker, yes? There is only one Rodon?" He asked.

Rodon laughed. "You have known me my whole life and you wonder now if there are other men named Rodon?"

He blushed. "Well..." He started, very unlike him. "While it is true that I have known thee all of my life, you have always been just another man passing through. I have not conversed with thee ever... But I believe I heard your name the other day from a friend of mine at the tavern."

"Oh? Pray tell," said Rodon.

"Climaticus, the Lydian. He told me that you helped him find work at one of your forges. He was ever grateful for not only did you give him work, but some new work clothes and lodgings. He was ever grateful, and I did not know if this was you or another man." Bartha concluded.

"Although I do not know the name, I do know that I am the only Rodon the spear-maker, though I confess it has been a few years since I bent over the smelter. And this does sound like a practice that I employ. If I find men suitable in the markets, I will hire them. If they are poor, I will offer the things you mentioned as terms of labor."

Bartha's face brightened. "Yes, then it must be you. Climaticus is a man of sunset colored hair and a small scar on his upper lip. You would know him."

Rodon's eyes widened. "Why yes, I do know this man. He is still young and has a very large back? For he is a solid worker and I do think he has a good head on his shoulders."

"The same man." Bartha smiled.

"I do the same for all my men, for I am a just employer. If any man need, and by meeting his needs, I can have a healthier and happier worker, then meet those needs I do. And as I recall now, Climaticus is an orphan here, for his parents were killed by raiders? He had nothing to begin with. By blessing those who have naught, we bless our own futures." Rodon said.

"Go in." Bartha said. "I will wager the master is most ready, for he has heard us talking all this while." Rodon entered the shop. Tryphon was hustling here and there, putting things in bags and boxes. Rodon eyed him with amusement.

"I sought to buy all the merchandise good Tryphon. That includes all of the trappings that went with it." Rodon said with a smile.

Tryphon stopped. "I did not know you were coming so early friend."

"So you wanted to cheat me a little?" Rodon asked.

"Not so..." Tryphon stopped. "Well. Not cheat. But I did not know if you would notice a few things missing here and there." He straightened up from a box where he dropped a small wrapped cloth.

"What was that you dropped then?" Rodon asked. He walked over and unbound the cloth. In it was a small hammer and chisel, for writing on the tablets. "And this is this not part of the business?"

And so, until the sun stood overhead Rodon and Tryphon went through of the items in the shop. Rodon allowing him to take personal items but not those that would be tied to the business. They worked a while longer, loading things into a cart beside the house in the street. Tryphon's wife was surprised that Rodon helped. He packed so efficiently, even organizing the boxes and bags and baskets as they went onto the cart. The packing concluded, Rodon and Tryphon went back into the shop.

"Though I know the answer and you have decided it, yet I would like for you to tell me plainly oh, son of my old friend. You have decided to sell me your shop and it's land and all the loans and assets that are associated with it? For I would like to hear it out of your mouth." Rodon asked plainly.

"Yes, yes, yes! All is yours! But I must be on the road and there is the matter of your payment!" Tryphon said, exhaustedly. "We have been at this all morning, making sure you are satisfied."

"I will pay, and pay gladly. See? Even now, my men are coming, along with one of the King's record keepers." Rodon went outside, where three men were working a cart towards the house. It was piled with boxes and must have been very heavy, from the way they were moving. Beside the men was another man, dressed in the manner of the Kings scribes, for he was one of them.

Rodon motioned for Tryphon to come and look.

"What is in the boxes?" Tryphon asked.

"You will see." Rodon said, handing Tryphon a small bronze knife. "Cut the red string, if you please."

Tryphon cut the red string of the box Rodon had his hand on and stepped back.

Rodon unlatched it, opening the lid. Inside were long slender bars of the precious metal, all of them stamped with the Kings signet. "All bars are properly weighed and measured. All boxes are bound with the red string. This box has 100 bars in it. There are ten boxes here. This is my valuation of your business. For I know more of your business than you, Tryphon. For before I went home that night, I visited the King's record keepers and ask of your accounts. They valued you at 900 bars. So then this box of 100 is for the business, effects and land of this place. There are ten total boxes on the cart." Rodon went to the scribe who had a bag on his neck.

The man took from out of his bag a large tablet, one with the King's signet.

"Here is a king's tablet of ownership. Simply read it and make your mark at the bottom. The King's scribe will return it to the records hall and a copy will be made. This done you will be rid of the whole of it. All of the gold on the cart for all that remains here. All the gold on the cart for the sale." Rodon held the tablet for him to carve his name upon it.

Tryphon looked at the cart, Rodon, the tablet, his cart and then back to Rodon.

"I cannot count all that now. And there is no way under the gods sky that I can carry it now either." How do I know that you will not hire men to come steal it from me once I am beyond the city gates? And lo, look now, there are men about us walking to and fro on their own journeys that do look at this cart and that, and have begun thinking to themselves the same things." Tryphon was visibly worried and his hands were trembling.

"Worry not good friend. Read this tablet, sign it, and take but some of the gold now and go to your new lodging. Return when you can and all the remainder of the gold will be safely stored here, in your old house... With interest. Read and sign" Rodon held the tablet for him to make his mark again.

Tryphon looked to his wife who was at the backside of Rodon's cart, looking at the gold. She gingerly took one of the bars and bit it.

"It is real." Rodon said.

"Indeed," she said, and placed the bar back. Tryphon made his mark, threw himself at the box and tried to lift it out of the cart but found he could not.

"Come Tryphon," Rodon said. "Take your gold, I will take care of these boxes. They will remain unbroken and sealed in their own vault if you choose to retrieve them."

Tryphon nodded and was quickly gone. Rodon handed one of the men the tablet. Placing it in a small bag around his neck, Rodon instructed him to be quick and to return at good speed. The man started running at a good pace, in the direction of the King's palace.

"What of these?" The man leading the cart asked. "Take them all inside. We shall build a new vault to hold them." Rodon said.

It was three moons later that Tryphon returned to Babylon. He came into town on his own, in a hurry. He was rude with the gatekeeper for he said He had pressing business that could not wait and the gatekeeper must stand aside. He galloped through the streets when he could, kicking up dust and bothering everyone he passed. He was mounted on a large white horse with purple and silver tack. It was lavishly adorned, as was Tryphon. He was a bit reddened, for he had been in the sun more in this last month than he had been in five years, but his black and silver clothed robes were splendid nonetheless. He approached his old house but passed right by it for he did not recognize it. Instead of the single house and store he had left, there stood a two story structure, made of royal brick. It was gleaming white and had large windows on the second floor. The first floor had many windows but were smallish and high, enough to let light in, but not large enough for even a child to fit through, let alone a thief. He reined his horse and went inside.

The walls were massive and the door was thick and made of wood and hung open. Inside were four men who worked at four tables in the middle of the room. Besides a small eating area, there was nothing else in the room but one door in the back. The walls were also gleaming white and high and on them were decorations. Tryphon recognized the decorations them as the tokens that were once in the box. He saw the rare gold bracelet, the Bronze neck piece, the scarlet cloth, and the turquoise beetle and many more. Underneath the first, were the names of those who owed, and the amount that was owed. He did not see names under the others, for he did not recognize them, and it seemed that they must not be so delinquent. At the back, above the door, was the token box lid, that, now free of its box, hung on the wall as a placard. "Better a little caution than a great regret" it read.

"Greetings friend!" a cheerful voice inquired. A smallish man with a well-trimmed square beard greeted him. He was in a white linen, like the priests.

"Ah. Umm..." Started Tryphon. "I wonder if Rodon the spear maker is here?"

"He is away on business at the moment. How might I help you?" The man asked.

"I am Tryphon, son of Mathon. I have gold on account here and I wish to withdraw some of it."

"And your token?" the man asked, pointing to the wall.

Tryphon was visibly disturbed that this man did not know who he was.

"You are standing in it!" he cried. "For this is my house!" He was furious. The man did not know who he was? This was an insult. "Find Rodon now and tell him that I demand my gold!"

Messengers had been sent and It was after a little while that Rodon came through the front door. He was clean shaven and in a spotless garment. He greeted Tryphon with gladness.

"Ah Tryphon my good friend! Look how well rested and tanned from the sun you are! I see that my servants have given you some soup and some refreshments after your journey from Sippar. Have you need of anything else?"

"I come to collect my gold!"

Rodon straightened his robes. "Let us sit. For though you have had refreshment, I have not, and I would like some." So saying, Rodon directed Tryphon to the seating area. He spoke quickly to one of the men, who hurried out of the front door. He then joined Tryphon at the eating area.

Once Rodon was seated and a drink poured for him, he began speaking.

"It was early that morning that I arrived to see you, do you recall?" Rodon asked. Before Typhon could answer Rodon continued. "And it was early that you were packing. Both of us were in a hurry that day, but I think that you were more hurried than I was, for I recall taking my time making sure that all I desired was in order. Two tablets did I bring that day. The first tablet you signed. The second tablet remained in the bag of the man who was with the cart... And you read neither... Tell me, out of curiosity, I trust your journey to Sippar was uneventful? For before you answer know this, that I hired men to follow you at a distance to ensure your safety. They told me that you met no one with ill intent on your way there. When they had reported this to me, I hired them out again to ensure you were not robbed during your stay there."

Tryphon stared with amazement. "There were men watching me that whole time?"

"Truly they continue to watch you," Rodon said. "They tell me of the lavish lifestyle that you have grown accustomed to all this while. I cannot imagine that you have spent 100 bars of gold during this time, however."

Tryphon was angry. "You should not have men watching me Rodon. That smacks of treachery."

"It was twice that I asked you to read the contract. If you care to recall I told you that the box we looked in was full of gold. I also told you that there were other boxes on the cart. There were nine other boxes on the cart. I asked you to read and sign the tablet for the sale of your business and all its effects for 100 bars. Recall what I said: 'The King's treasurers valued you at 900 bars. This box of 100 is for the business, the effects and land of this place."

Tryphon did not understand.

"There were ten boxes on the cart." Rodon continued, "The one I showed you had one hundred bars of gold. Tell me, how many bars of gold were on the cart?"

"There were 1000 bars of gold on the cart." Tryphon objected. "900 of them are yet mine!"

Rodon motioned for one of the men to come over to where they were.

"Bring out the nine boxes that we stored here three months ago." Rodon commanded.

"Sir, they are all still within the new vault." The man said, bowing.

"Yes, so they are!" Rodon hopped up. "Come let us go see them!"

They went through the door to the back area where there were crates and bags, neatly ordered. In the Middle of the room was a small depression. It was decorated and sealed. There was a tablet embedded into the floor that read: "Do not open until the return of the owner, Son of Mathon.

A man entered into the back room from the front. "I have done as you commanded." He said and stepped out of the way. A prominent man, dressed with the colors of the King stepped forward. He was from the royal treasury.

"Ah Narplu Arad, my friend! Did you bring the signed tablet?" Rodon asked, bowing.

"Yes honorable Rodon, here it is. What are your purposes? For truth be told, this is the copy that you paid for, after it was delivered three moons ago. The original is still with the king's records." Said the Scribe.

"But this copy has the King's seal? It is official?" Rodon asked.

"Just as the first one." The Scribe said.

"Hand it to this man." Rodon said. "Read it Tryphon."

Tryphon took the tablet and read it. "And so? What does this prove other than what I have stated? That all the gold in the boxes are mine!"

"Open the vault." Rodon commanded his men. So, striking the tablet first, and handing the fragments to the scribe, they broke out the floor so they could remove the boxes. One by one they carefully took them out, being cautious not to break the red strings still around them. Once laid at the feet of Tryphon, Rodon waited. "Well?" Said Tryphon.

Rodon handed him a small bronze knife.

"Cut the string." Rodon said.

Tryphon took the knife, bent down and cut the red string. His hands were trembling. Once cut, he flung down the knife, breathed deep, opened the top of the box to behold within, large quantities of brown dusty rocks.

It was during the early evening at the Temple of Learning that Narplu Arad, the scribe who worked for the King caught up with Rodon. Rodon was drinking a spiced wine and eating some figs by one of the great columns outside the Temple. He looked lost in thought as Narplu Arad approached him.

"I pray that I am not interrupting you?" Narplu Arad asked. "For you look as though you stand on a shoreline, waiting for your ship to return."

Rodon smiled and put down the figs. "Not so. Just thinking of you and many other men that I might perchance encounter here tonight. The great Nomasir is scheduled to speak but he has not arrived yet, or I would be inside already."

Narplu Arad opened his mouth to speak but Rodon already knew what he would ask.

"You are going to ask about Tryphon and the boxes are you not?" Rodon smiled.

"Even so," Narplu Arad asked.

"Come inside then, and I will discuss it at length." Rodon said, and picking up his figs he went in.

The great hall was busy with men and women from all over. It had become even busier these last few years since Sargon had been busy north of Nineveh, building his great palace. The king had not been in Babylon in some time, but the merchants and traders had not been idle. New trade with Nineveh was opening more and more doorways to greater and greater wealth.

"Behold Rodon! The richest bronze worker in Babylon!" cried a man near the front. "We have been waiting on your arrival!"

Rodon smiled at Narplu Arad. "Not will I discuss this with you privately my friend. For I am the substitute speaker for Nomasir. Come, sit at the front and I should address all of your questions in my speech." Rodon took Narplu Arad by the hand, as was the custom with close friends, and led him to the front center, to a small pillow, so that he may sit.

Walking to the small platform, Rodon too, sat and addressed the audience for quiet. This having been achieved he started his speech.

"My good friend Narplu Arad, the King's scribe has been seated at the front of this great chamber because most my explanations of my dealings with Tryphon, the son of our most esteemed Mathon will be directed at him. But as is the custom, I will share with you some truths that I have learned along the way. And some, from very surprising sources."

"I begin by setting your mind at ease. Some most undoubtedly, have heard the tale of my dealings with Tryphon and how I am called a cheat and a scoundrel by him. I will tell you that this is not so. For a fool and his money soon find a quarrel amongst themselves and they quickly part ways. Such was the case with Tryphon. Let me ask you as a group, how many of you dealt with the honorable Mathon, while he was still with us?"

Many people raised their hands or stood, to show they had.

"Thank you. And those who are raising their hands please stand." Rodon said.

They did so, and all those men looked at one another, as did the group. It was around one quarter of all those assembled.

Rodon continued. "Now of those standing, please remain standing if you also dealt with Tryphon, his son."

Most of the men sat, only three remained. One of the three suddenly slapped his head and sat down.

"Why did you sit?" Rodon asked him.

"Because I confess that I only finished my business with Mathon after he died. I did not any business with his son, but only paid the loan back to him. I see this in my mind as not doing business with Tryphon." He said.

"I would agree. You were honoring your word with Mathon. And that is indeed honorable. Many would have taken the cheats way and gone to Tryphon declaring the deal moot and no money owed." Rodon said, pleased. "I commend you for this. Tell me, what is your name? For I now also seek to do business with you, seeing your honor."

"Plarkus the stone layer," the man said. "And you already have done business with me Rodon, for I built your new store where was old Mathon's!"

The room laughed. Rodon smiled. "All the better." He said. "And did I pay you?"

"Yes!" said Plarkus. "You were prompt with your payment. But it was not me you paid. You paid Gramad and he paid me."

"Ah yes, this man I do know. He also is a just builder." Rodon admitted.

"Now, to these two men still standing, How is it that you continued in your business with Tryphon?" Rodon asked.

"I confess it was out of need." The first man said. "I am Aratamesh, from Ur. I had arrived late and the Kings Treasury was closed. The innkeeper did not want my silver so I was forced to go to Tryphon to exchange currency. The man was fair, or so I thought at the time, but I only used him once."

Rodon asked, "Why only once?"

"Because of his high prices!" Aratamesh yelled angrily. "His tax was far larger than any in the city."

"Thank you," Rodon said, "please take your leisure. And the man sat down.

"And you fine lady?" Rodon addressed the last person standing. "Why did you use Tryphon?"

"Because he offered the same terms as his father." She said plainly.

"Nothing more?" Rodon asked.

"No. The man did not want to honor my agreement with Mathon, but I forced him to keep his word." She said.

"Forced him?" Rodon asked.

"I told him most unashamedly that I would tell of one his daughter's exploits with my sons were he not honest." She said, pridefully. "My sons are temple incense carriers. Our family has had that contract ere since my father's father started it. His oldest daughter, I forget her name, tried to steal some but my sons chased her down.

She was repentant so they did not tell the guards, but some was destroyed. I confess I was hard on them for I made them work double until the remainder was restored." After this, she sat down.

"Might I ask you more questions?" Rodon asked.

"Certainly," she said, from her seat, not bothering to arise again.

"Your job is delivery only of the goods to the temple?" Rodon asked.

"No, we grow and harvest what we can, and buy from traders the rest. We then prepare it ourselves. The chief priests takes them and burns them as is their practice. When there is lack, we must buy. Often is there lack of myrrh, anise and poppy. The preparations of Marduk are different than that of Tiamat or Nergal or Shemesh, so they must all be done individually. It is a very dedicated job and our family takes great pride in it."

"And you borrowed from Tryphon?" Rodon asked.

"Three times. At the same rates as Mathon's." She said, her nose screwing up, "I do not know why the man demanded such a raise in rates. We had a good bargain… Why ruin it?"

"Thank you for your honesty," Rodon said smiling. "I am happy you were all so forthcoming. And strangely, I can find no fault with your dealings with him. For he was a man consumed with fear and greed. And this is my first point I will make this evening. That the greediest man is the poorest man, and the richest man is the one who gives the most."

"My second point is related by somewhat backwards on the face. For though greed makes you horde and become dishonest... Also saving is for the poor minded and fearful. And the opposite is true as well. Investing is for the rich... Or those who are deemed by fortune to become rich. So we see the poor have two things in common. They are greedy and fearful, sitting on their gold, having to touch it with lusty fingers to make sure it is not going anywhere. Likewise, the rich give away when it is needed and are not afraid to let the gold go out on its own and work for them. And I tell you the truth, this was the case of Tryphon and myself, as my good friend Ando here will tell you; He is my guest here tonight."

Ando stood, for he was also on the front row. He was not sure how to begin and fumbled with his fingers for a little while.

"Begin with the passing of Mathon." Rodon suggested.

"Yes. Mathon died." Ando started.

"This much we already know!" Cried a man from the back.

"But not before allowing Ando to buy his freedom!" Rodon called, saving Ando the embarrassment. "He stands before you a free man!" Most did not know this, and they were quiet. Freedom was something these men took for granted.

"Tell us most honorable Ando, how much did your freedom cost?" Rodon asked.

"5 gold. And 5 for my wife and 5 for my son." Ando answered.

All were amazed. That this man saved that much could not be believed.

"And how did you acquire the gold?" Rodon asked.

"I worked for it." Ando answered.

"And..." Rodon probed.

"And more work?" Ando replied.

Some laughed.

"But we all know this is such a large sum." Rodon said. "How did it multiply so quickly."

"Oh, he kept if for me, as investment." Ando said.

The men around the room listened but no more was forthcoming. Rodon thought they might understand, but as they did not, he beckoned to them again.

"Come! All those that borrowed from Mathon, stand again!" He cried.

They stood, as did Rodon and stepped down beside Ando.

"And did you know that you were borrowing from a slave?" Rodon asked.

The men murmured and looked at one another.

"No probably not the exact gold that Ando had in the safekeeping of his master, but still, were it not for those who trusted Mathon to keep their gold, he would not have any to lend out!" Rodon thrust Ando's hand into the air.

"Behold men, the richest lender in Babylon. For he came from debt into freedom and just yesterday, I have helped find him a house of his own. He has a prospering security business and is currently seeking clients of his own. He and I have left on good terms. I have purchased his house on old Mathon's property and increased my storage for other's gold. But were it not for him, people like Mathon and myself would have no business." He let Ando's arm down and went back to the platform. He would speak again but men had surrounded Ando, asking him about his rates and his men and his contracts. Ando was beside himself, giddy with the prospect of all the work.

Narplu Arad took this opportunity to approach Rodon.

"I thought you were going to tell us about your dealings with Tryphon." He asked.

"Can't you see that I am?" Rodon laughed. "I did not expect to incite such a mob of customers on poor Ando here."

Narplu Arad took the stage then. "Please, please, good people. I do have honest questions of Rodon. Will you assault the good sentry-man at a later time? I would hear Rodon finish!"

They heard him, and though there were strained whispers, the din had quieted just enough to allow Rodon to continue.

"So then! I will tell you my third rule of the flow of wealth that stems from the first two... For I have found that when I give to the moon, it comes back as the sun. When I treat others with kindness, eventually kindness will flow back to me. That if I cast my bread upon the water, soon it will return with every wave. For there are hundreds that I have helped and the kindness is never lost. If I give in parcels, parcels of goodness will find me... But the second part of this law bears hearing as well. I do not just scatter my seeds to the wind. There is a difference in specific planting and foolish waste."

He paused to let them listen for though he was speaking long, one by one, the room was filling up, as others came by to listen.

"I will say that last part again. Foolish altruism is not love. For love is action with purpose. If I love my friend, I will help him to succeed. I will not buy him strong drink but will help him avoid strong drink. If you are wiser than your friend, direct him in the path he needs to travel... Not in the path he thinks he should travel. And this is the same for children and parents. Train them in the way they should go, not in the way they want to go."

"Say to your future wife or husband: I will love thee more than today's wife or husband." He pointed to a rich Mede man and woman who stood by one of the columns. "Do you wish to cheat your old wife of her blessing? Then spend all your money now on her. Do you wish to bless the wife of your old age? Then invest while you are yet young. Tithe towards your elder spouse... And if you do not have a spouse... Get a spouse!"

Those with their spouses poked each other while those there by themselves looked around for their friends who they knew to still be unmarried.

"Now, I have three more things on my list to tell you of my laws of the flow of wealth. So I will tell you the first two bluntly and then address the third by itself, for it has to do with my dealings with the son of Mathon, which I am sure many of you are here to hear. And for those of you just now coming in, no I am not Nomasir, for he is much wealthier than I am. I am simply Rodon, a spear maker."

"The wealthiest spear maker in Babylon!" A woman cried out.

"Most worthy of listening to!" Another cried.

"A fine and honorable man!" Yet another cried.

Rodon waved his hands before any more flattery spilled from their lips.

"And I will tell you a story of spear making if you will let me!" Rodon called out.

"It was near the beginning of my life, just a boy, yet working diligently at the bronze furnace. A merchant from Tushpa with a large fur hat came visiting selling tongs and shovels and the like along with his copper. He was a smallish man with a dancing frame. I will never forget him. Nor will I forget his tools that fell apart the day after he left. The master's rage was so that he would have found the man and beat him to death were he still in Babylon. But the trader had sold the day he was leaving, for we never saw him again. So he devised a way for us to make our own tools. And two lessons will draw from this story, for it was the first two things that I learned of wisdom, ere before this temple stood. The first is this: I am too poor to buy poor tools. The second is similar. Having a good tool is good, but better still is having the tool that makes that tool."

"And now I shall tell you of Tryphon and my dealings with him. For Narplu Arad and some other of my friends believe that I cheated him. I will tell it plainly and then answer questions." Rodon said. And so saying this, he relayed the whole story. When he was done he took questions.

"You say you had two tablets with you. What did the other one say?" Asked a tall black skinned woman with a large yellow head-dress.

"That I would take the rocks back and pay him 500 bars." Said Rodon. "For if you recall I did ask him three or four times to read the tablet.

They murmured amongst themselves.

"But you said that all the boxes were gold!" Said a man.

"Think back." Rodon said. "I told him that this one box had 100 bars and that there were ten boxes in total. Did I tell him of the contents of the other boxes?"

No one answered.

"Did I not suggest that he but take a small handful of bars and put the rest with me to gain the interest? And did Tryphon ever actually give me a price for his shop? And when he complained about the separation of the business and the house that I offered a goodly sum to buy the whole lot? I paid them on the spot the fifty pieces of gold in my wallet even then and there. And this is but one half of a bar of gold. So in all, they got from me one hundred and one half bars. The bars were of a sure weight and measure for on gold melting days we have the King's scribes there to account for our weight. If anything, we over pour, such is our counting. Never a bar goes out light, but we will smelt it and pour it again. Do you all not know this? How many have ever gotten a light bar from me?"

No one raised their hand, but one man in the middle stood.

"I can attest for this. For once I took a Rodon Bar to the exchangers and they let me have it on a 1:1 ratio for the gold value of silver shekels. Never has a private exchanger done this for me for free, and so I asked why it was this way, and he laughed and said: 'If Rodon poured it, then I will always have a surplus.'"

"But you said you would pay him ten times the amount of Mathon's business!" A man standing near the outside said.

"Nay! I said 'this business' not the one of his father's." Rodon countered. "For we all know Tryphon's business was failing. His father had been wise, but the son was a worrisome fool. Let me ask you: How much rent did Tryphon charge Ando for the house at the back of the property? And how much did he pay them?" He motioned for Ando to stand again. "Tell them yourself."

"I paid nothing in rent and I was paid a good deal more than double the rate of guard." Ando said, and sat down.

"Free rent!" a man cried. "Were I to live there, I would be rich already!"

Rodon laughed. "It seemed the servant was wiser than the master, for the house Ando bought yesterday is twice as large as Tryphon's. Now, I do not Ando did anything wrong, for he never asked to be treated with such luxury, and did his job well. But it was Tryphon who was a poor steward of his own money and Ando was the recipient of the result of misspending." He motioned to his friend once again. "You did nothing wrong dear Ando, and I am glad for your prosperity."

Rodon stood up and addressed them all. "If there are no more questions for me on my manner of handling Tryphon and the purchase of his business, I would like to give to you my last lesson on the law of the flow of wealth, for this lesson is the reason I came up with this name. The law of the flow of wealth is just the opposite that we see from our beautiful Euphrates river. It is that wealth flows uphill, against all logic, and I will tell you why. For wealth is never lost, it is simply transferred. Wealth never disappears; it simply goes into the hands of the more wealthy. Test this and see if it is true."

"Is it not true that most customers are poorer than the shopkeepers?"

"Is it not true that most wealthy seek to do business with other wealthy?"

"Is it not true that the wealthier the shopkeeper, the wealthier the client?"

"Is it not true that garbage wages purchase garbage goods?"

"Is it not true that the ones buying food at the market stalls work at the markets?"

"Is it not true that in times of crises, those who have more wealth gain and those who have not, lose already what they have?

"I make this plea to you to understand wealth. For wealth is not a mystery. It is as Arkad spoke many years ago, and even as Nomasir teaches us with their 'Seven Cures for a Lean Purse' and their 'Five Laws of Gold.' And what do we know about the commonality of both of these laws? That the first law and cure are the same. Pay thyself first. Set it aside to gain for tomorrow. Invest this instead of spending it now. Steal from your wife today to provide for her in her advanced years. Take gold away now to have gold give to you later."

"This is the power of the rich. That they care not what their neighbor's think of their new chariot or their garden... That they do not look like the King. But they look like everyone else, for their gold does not lie with them, for their gold has departed from them and is working in their name, at another destination."

"Think not that gold is a crutch... Think that gold is a child of your labor. Know that it is as obedient as you direct it to be. Do not throw gold to the wind recklessly, but place it into places where you know you will succeed. And when you give gold, do not give grudgingly, but give cheerfully, for wisdom will show you what is good soil to sow into."

"These are my Laws of the Flow of Wealth."

"The greediest man is the poorest man and the richest man is he who gives the most."

"Saving money is for the fearful. Investing money is for the wise."

"Direct kindness is not the same as foolish altruism."

"Tithe toward your elder spouse... And get a spouse."

"Keep the tool. But better gain the tool that makes that tool,"

"For, you are too poor to own poor tools."

"And lastly, Wealth is never lost. It is simply transferred upwards."

Rodon stood on the stage breathless. He had poured out his heart to the people of his city in the room, and now, even the people standing on the portico, outside the room… For there were more here now than he had ever seen before. His thoughts were hazy but he was still fired up in his belly. His hands, old and tough from the bronze forge had many calluses still on them. He slapped them together, making a noise so loud that it made most of them jump.

"What are the cures for a lean purse?" He asked them.

1) Start thy purse to fattening. Pay thyself first.
2) Control thy expenditures.
3) Make thy gold multiply.
4) Guard thy treasures from loss.
5) Make of thy dwelling a profitable investment.
6) Insure a future income.
7) Increase thy ability to earn.

He clapped again. "And what are the five rules of gold?"

1) Gold comes easily and in increasing quantity to the person who saves at least 1/10th of their earnings.
2) Gold labors diligently and multiplies for the person who finds it profitable employment.

3) Gold clings to the protection of the person who invests their gold with wise people.
4) Gold slips away from the person who invests gold into purposes through which they are not familiar.
5) Gold flees the person who tries to force it into impossible earnings.

He smiled and bowed. The crowd cheered him and waved their scarfs in adoration at his speech. The room, acoustics perfect to let one man be heard by hundreds, seemed to echo thunder at the applause. Eventually, someone threw a flower to the small stage, and then, someone threw a shekel. Soon, it was raining coins all about him. Copper, Silver, and Gold came pouring down like rain as the crowd rained down on him the metals he had loved his whole life.

And so was written in the "Chronicles of the Wisdom of Gold" Rodon's "Seven Laws of the Flow of Wealth" along with Kobbi's "Seven Tablets of Earning" and many, many others.

5

The Principles Discussed in The Richest Man in Babylon

Laws of Handling Wealth

1) Live on less than you earn
2) Seek advice from those that are competent enough to give it
3) Learn how to make money work for you

Seven Cures for a Lean Purse

1) Start thy purse to fattening. Pay thyself first.
2) Control thy expenditures.
3) Make thy gold multiply.
4) Guard thy treasures from loss.
5) Make of thy dwelling a profitable investment.
6) Insure a future income.
7) Increase thy ability to earn.

Good Luck

1)Good luck will follow those who answer the call of opportunity.

2) Procrastination steals your wealth.

The Five Rules of Gold

1) Gold cometh gladly and in increasing quantity to any man who will put by not less than one-tenth of his earnings to create an estate for his future and that of his family.

2) Gold laboreth diligently and contentedly for the wise owner who finds for it profitable employment, multiplying even as the flocks of the field.

3) Gold clingeth to the protection of the cautious owner who invests it under the advice of men wise in its handling.

4) Gold slippeth away from the man who invests it in businesses or purposes with which he is not familiar or which are not approved by those skilled in its keep.

5) Gold flees the man who would force it to impossible earnings or who followeth the alluring advice of tricksters and schemers or who trusts it to his own inexperience and romantic desires in investment.

Other Lessons

1) Better a little caution than a great regret.
2) We cannot afford to be without adequate protection.
3) Where the determination is, a way can be found.
4) Let hard work become your friend.

6

Principles Discussed
In this Book

Tablets of the Wisdom of Wealth

1) The work you do should make you happy.

2) The less flash you have, the less flash others see.

3) You become the average of the people you listen to.

4) Any hobby that does not serve to gain your wealth helps to deplete it.

5) Whatever your mind dwells on, your money flows in that direction

6 Without the preservation of knowledge, what you have can be quickly stolen from you.

7) Take away choice by promoting competition. Demand grows on goodwill. Marketability is supported by desire.

The 7 Tablets of Earning

1) Know who holds the vault-stone (good debt vs bad debt).

2) Know who holds the purse-string (who is able to pay).

3) Know who holds the iron dagger (those who prey on you).

4 Know who holds the chariot reigns (those who control your money).

5) Know who holds the counting stones (book keeping).

6) Know who holds the keys (those few people who know everyone and can open every door).

7) Know who you owe (your debt is the quickest way to lose your earnings).

The Laws of the Flow of Wealth

1) The greediest man is the poorest man and the richest man is he who gives the most.

2) Saving money is for the fearful. Investing money is for the wise.

3) Direct kindness is not the same as foolish altruism.

4) Tithe toward your elder spouse… And get a spouse.

5) Keep the tool. But better gain the tool that makes that tool.

6) You are too poor to own poor tools.

7) Wealth is never lost. It is simply transferred upwards.

Thank You

Whether or not you gain actual gold coins in your life is not the point of this book, Clason's book, or any story in either book. Grow with what you have. Learn more ways to invest. Get, and get well, learn and prosper. But remember, in all your getting of wealth and knowledge; do not forget to get wisdom. For if knowledge is the facts of the thing, then wisdom is how to apply it to your life.

You may be poor, middle class, or rich. Money does not care. That's the glory of money. It is like Buoyancy and Density. What makes the clouds float are the same laws that let the ocean crash. Make your money becomeas fluid as water, so that if you need to fly or settle, it may. Do not follow the advice of idiots, even if you are seen as one. Follow your training and your mind. For if you follow your heart or others "great ideas," you will be surely overtaken with calamity.

Trust that all things work together for the good of those that love God and are called according to His purposes. The purpose of wealth is to bless those around you. Yourself, your family, your friends, and those you invest in. Remember, don't despise a penny – pennies make up dollars.

Pauly Hart
April 7, 2021